Firm
Denial

Licia Flynn

Published by Klar Marketing Communications

ISBN: 978-1-7322777-3-1

CONTENTS

CHARACTER INDEX

Sara — Friend of Lana in Shanghai, flight attendant at Emirates

PROLOGUE

The sky seemed impossibly black as I ran through the unkempt fields of rural China. The wind sliced my cheeks while blades of grass cut my legs.

My heart raced. I was breathless while trying to discern shapes in the distance.

During my flight, I'd abandoned my purse but held onto my bag. I kept the carrier close to my chest and could hear my cat, Peter's troubled breathing. He too was petrified, and fear had frozen him.

Within thick layers of fog, I could finally see the plane. I continued to run as fast as I could, while Peter whimpered.

If I didn't move faster, if I failed to reach the aircraft, then everything I'd ever worked for would be lost.

I yelled, "Wait for me. Please don't go!"

I stumbled in the dark while clutching Peter's soft body of fur. With what adrenaline remained, I shouted again at the top of my lungs. But it was pointless because no one could see or hear me.

"Please don't leave," I screamed as an enormous blow struck my head. Dizziness overwhelmed me. I fell to the ground, and everything became blurry.

PART 1

CHAPTER 1
Houston, Texas — 2018
Aaron Walker

I sat in the middle of my psychiatrist's office, not sure what to say. Dr. Lee's receding hairline mirrored his passion.

There was no way he'd ever get me, let alone be able to help me. However, seeing Lee was a requirement because if I didn't get my medication, I couldn't sleep. If I didn't sleep, then I wouldn't function.

The office was grim with old furniture: orange seats, pinewood paneling, and green carpets. Stacks of yellowed paper were piled high on Lee's oak desk. Medical and psychology books crammed a shelf in the corner.

I stared out the window into the parking lot. Anxious mothers impatiently persuaded their ADD kids to climb into the back seats of their SUVs. The setting sun cast dark shadows across the concrete pavement.

Sitting in his leather chair, Lee barely looked at me. He

furiously scribbled notes, but finally glanced up. With a blank expression, he asked, "How are you, Aaron?"

Like you care, I thought. "Alright."

"Have you been taking your meds?"

"Yep."

"How've you been sleeping?"

"Like shit."

For a split second, Lee looked genuinely concerned. "Aaron is there anything you care to discuss?"

"What?"

"You're taking your meds. You're following my orders. Maybe you need more therapy and less medication."

"Yeah, that's what I've been saying," I snapped.

Dr. Lee raised his head and asked hopefully, "Are you ready to talk about Iraq?"

"Nope."

"Are you sure?" he asked tilting his head to the side.

"Yeah, I'm sure. Stop asking!"

"Whoa, I'm sensing a lot of aggression," Lee stated in his typically cool, condescending manner.

"Yep."

"I think we need to add an antipsychotic to your cocktail."

"Whatever," I muttered jumping up.

"Aaron, where are you going? We're not finished!"

As I stormed through Lee's dusty waiting room, I was caught off guard by a young brunette sitting on the old, brown sofa.

She looked sophisticated because of her green suit which emphasized her pale white skin, thick black lashes, and full lips. She pretended not to notice me as I barged out the front door.

I wanted to stop and ask her name. Or find out what she was reading. But I was too tense.

CHAPTER 2

It was Friday afternoon, and I was back in Lee's dirty cage.

The only good thing about these routine office visits was the hope I might run into *the* mysterious woman again.

Lee acted as if nothing had happened. He scribbled notes like a zombie.

"The loser took me for everything and ran off."

Lee nodded. "Your business partner?"

"Yes, my partner!"

"Please continue."

"Yeah, so if it weren't for this bastard, I'd be out of the red."

Lee stopped writing, raised his head and clarified, "You mean debt?"

"Yeah, I've filed for bankruptcy."

"Aaron, is it only your business you're upset about?"

"Yeah."

"What about your family?"

"My wife left me years ago."

"How did that affect you?"

I shrugged. "Not much of a marriage."

"Okay, so how's the new medication working?"

"It's fine …"

"Good, good, these new medications are experimental, but they're supposed to help."

"Which company makes these antidepressants?"

"Why?"

"I just want to know," I demanded.

With a sigh, Lee replied, "Steiger Pharmaceuticals."

***

After weeks of pointless sessions with Lee, I'd almost forgotten about the pretty brunette. Then one evening, I was heading down the gravel path towards the parking lot when I heard the distinct sound of high heels. The clicking grew louder as a woman turned the corner, and I could smell a feminine scent — a floral fragrance.

I was startled to see *her* again and mumbled something.

She stopped, looked me in the eye, and asked, "Sorry, what did you say?"

I swallowed hard and replied, "The sound of your heels." I then clasped my hand against my chest and continued "As a guy, it's a sound I love. But as a woman, it must make you feel so powerful."

"Ah, well, these are just wedges," she said turning to show me her shoes "You should see my stilettos."

I grinned. "Yeah, I'll have to see them, sometime."

She suddenly became nervous and started to wobble which made me chuckle.

I exclaimed, "Hey, be careful!"

"Oh." Her cheeks reddened with embarrassment.

"Hey, you look great. Going somewhere special?"

"Not really. Just dinner with Dad."

"Your Dad?" I was surprised. She didn't look like she was going to meet her dad.

"Yeah." She nodded.

I took a deep breath. "Well, it was nice meeting you.

Have a great night."

She smiled back and said, "Bye, maybe I'll see you again?"

"Yeah, for sure."

I started to turn away, but then spun around and asked, "Hey, what's your name?"

"Helena," she responded while heading up the path.

"My name is Aaron," I shouted, but she was already out of earshot. I watched Helena head into my doctor's office.

I groaned. *So Lee was her dad?*

CHAPTER 3

A few weeks passed, but I hadn't seen Helena. I wondered what happened to her and was tempted to ask Lee about his daughter but didn't. I figured she'd eventually pop up.

I was used to attractive women. They generally responded to me. However, Helena looked at me with more intrigue than most. I'd already forgotten our conversation but couldn't stop thinking about how her eyes glimmered with curiosity.

I ran a cursory Internet search, but the only Helena Lee listed was in her eighties. I wondered if she'd given me her real name.

Then one night I was heading to my truck after my session with Lee. It was almost dark, and I dropped my keys. As I stumbled around looking for them under my vehicle, I heard the sound of clicking heels.

A woman laughed and asked, "What are you doing?"

I quickly jumped up and bashed my head against the undercarriage. "Ouch."

"Are you looking for these?" Helena playfully dangled keys from her hand and smiled as she watched me struggle to pull myself up.

"Yeah," I said grabbing the keys from her. "Here to see your dad?"

Helena shook her head and replied, "I have to get to class."

"What class?

"Ballet, it's across the street."

I nodded, as heavy silence filled the air. I didn't know what to say.

Then suddenly, Helena joked, "You'd make a great ballet dancer."

"Are you serious?"

"You look strong, yet you're very lean and perhaps lithe."

I raised an eyebrow. "Okay."

"It takes a lot of strength to be a ballerina," she explained.

Changing the subject, I suggested, "I'll walk you to your class."

"Thanks, but I can take care of myself."

"Look, this area is dangerous."

She paused for a moment. "Alright, if a criminal appears, I'll protect you."

"Very funny."

We slowly walked across the empty street to an even more deserted area.

Helena joked, "You should see how high I can kick."

"In those heels?" I asked skeptically.

We were now at the steps of a rundown building.

"I guess we're here," I observed. I was disappointed because I liked talking to Helena.

"We'll talk later" she promised, as if reading my mind.

"Aren't ballerinas supposed to be graceful?" I teased.

"Yes."

"You kind of had trouble with your heels when we first met."

She shrugged with a slight grin. "I guess you have that effect on women."

"Yeah, I hear that a lot," I joked.

CHAPTER 4

The following week I chased after Helena as she walked to her ballet class.

She turned to me and asked, "Do you get your exercise running after women?"

"Not exactly."

"Have you always been this athletic?" she teased.

"Actually, I got beat up a lot as a kid."

"By pretty blondes when you talked to other girls?"

"Ha, ha."

"Ah, so it was over who had the ball first or who got to be in charge?"

"Are you always this flirtatious with strangers?"

Helena tossed her hair to the side. "Only the ones with secrets to tell."

"What makes you think I have secrets?"

Helena continued walking. I followed slightly behind her. Suddenly she twirled around and exclaimed, "Okay, well then I have a story I'm dying to tell you."

"Okay."

"Meet me after class," she said with a sly grin.

***

I had to run errands. When I got back to Helena's studio, the lot was hazy, but lit by the moon so I could see that it was old and abandoned.

I felt anxious. Did she leave because I was late? But I wasn't. I'd only been gone an hour. Her class was ninety minutes long.

Angry, I frantically searched for Helena. I didn't sleep all night and was soaking in sweat.

By 8 a.m., I stormed over to Lee's office and pounded on his locked door. No one answered.

Sitting on the front doorsteps, I began to nod off. When I woke, Lee was shaking me.

"Aaron, what are you doing here?"

"Where is she?"

"Where is who?"

"Your daughter," I shouted.

Lee ignored my question and said, "Aaron, c'mon get up and come into my office."

I stumbled in and fell on the couch.

He offered me water and asked, "Aaron, when did you last take your meds?"

"Don't know. Can't remember."

"When did you last sleep?"

"Not sure."

"Have you been drinking?"

"Dr. Lee, where is she? I took Helena to her ballet class. She asked me to wait, but never returned."

"Aaron, I don't have a daughter."

"What do you mean you don't have a daughter?" I shouted.

The doctor raised his hand and said, "Calm down."

"Don't tell me to calm down. Where the hell is Helena?"

"Aaron, I have no daughter," Lee repeated.

"But that girl — that woman, I saw in your waiting room. I've seen her for weeks."

"What woman?"

"Tall, slender brunette, said you're her dad."

"Maybe there was a misunderstanding," Lee suggested.

"Yeah," I agreed.

"Where have you seen her?"

"Here, in the parking lot, and across the street."

Lee nodded and listened to me carefully.

I continued, "I followed her to the studio across the street."

"Aaron, the building across the street, burned down years ago."

"What?"

"Have you seen anyone else going over there?"

"Yeah, of course," I lied.

"Aaron, I think we need to adjust your medication."

"Doctor, you believe me, don't you? You know I've been seeing this woman, right?"

"Aaron, you're hallucinating."

"No doc, I'm not."

"We need to talk about Iraq."

"No, we don't," I stated flatly. "That was over ten years ago. I've moved on."

"Alright, then …"

The doctor paused as if he was afraid to say something. His reticence pissed me off.

"What?" I shouted.

"I think we need to discuss what happened in China and what *really* happened to Lana."

PART 2
CHINA — 2015

CHAPTER 1

Peter Lim stood by his private jet in an open field and anxiously scanned the area. It was the middle of the night, and the sky was dark except for a few scattered stars.

The pilot yelled, "Peter, c'mon we have to go."

"Please, I need another minute."

"No, we can't wait, let's go. *Gǎnkuài.*"

Peter reluctantly ascended the steps of his aircraft, pausing halfway up to peer into the distance. "I think I see something," he whispered.

"No Peter, it's your imagination."

"Please, wait. I hear something."

"We hear nothing. Let's go."

"But Lana said she would be here. She's never broken her word."

"Look, she's not here and we're long overdue."

"Please, just one more, minute," Peter implored.

"Peter, if we don't leave now, everything we've worked

for is jeopardized. Forget Lana. We need to go."

The crew grabbed Peter's arms, pulled him into the aircraft, and shut the door. Meanwhile, the pilot cranked up the engine and switched on the lights. The plane made a heavy sound as its exhaust system kicked up sand and dirt. It also sent dust billowing across the field.

Lim peered out the window on the side of the jet but saw only the darkness.

CHAPTER 2
Lana Hayaak

The sky seemed impossibly black and the air bone-chillingly cold as I ran through the unkempt fields of rural China. I felt the wind slice against my cheeks, and sharp blades of grass cut my bare legs. My heart raced, and I was breathless as I tried to discern shapes and objects in the distance.

During my flight, I'd abandoned my purse but held onto my bag. I kept the carrier close to my chest and could hear my cat, Peter's troubled breathing. He too was petrified, and fear had frozen him.

About a hundred feet away, I saw what appeared to be a plane. I surmised that it was my former boss, Peter Lim's private jet. After all, he and his team promised to meet me at this point.

Anxiety flowed through my veins. I was trapped in a nightmare where you desperately try to wake, but can't. I knew I was late and was practically paralyzed realizing I was close, yet so far away.

If only Lim knew what I'd gone through to get here, I thought as a burning sensation gripped my chest. Things hadn't been easy, but after leaving Aaron on the train, I was cornered by his client's thugs – glorified butchers.

I almost regretted poisoning Aaron because he had once promised: *Lana, if there's ever Armageddon, I'll protect you.* Then again, the trite platitudes of a drunken man are about as genuine as the promises of a politician. And, as always I was better off on my own.

Within thick layers of fog, I could finally see Lim's aircraft. I continued to scurry as fast as I could, while my furry friend panted loudly. My cat did his best to be strong, but he occasionally let out the sad whimpers of an animal in distress.

If I didn't move faster, if I failed to reach the safety of the plane, then everything I'd worked for would be lost.

I ran as fast as I could, in spite of the excruciating pain in my back. Earlier, when I first heard the blast and felt something tear through my shoulder, I assumed it was a bullet. Now, I realized that a dart filled with poison infected my body and would soon leave me paralyzed. I had drugged Aaron, and now the same fate had befallen me.

I was practically frozen as I yelled, "Peter, Peter, can you see me?"

I stumbled in the dark while clutching the soft body of my pet. With what adrenalin remained, I shouted at the top of my lungs. But it was pointless because Lim couldn't see or hear me.

"Please don't leave," I screamed as an enormous blow struck my head. Dizziness overwhelmed me as I fell to the ground and everything became blurry.

CHAPTER 3

Two thin, but heavily wrinkled migrant workers rifled through mountains of garbage somewhere in northwest China. Working tirelessly in the heat while immune to the scent of rotting sewage, they occasionally paused to swat bloated flies or to wipe drops of sweat from their leathery foreheads. The men persevered in the harsh conditions until seeing the soft contours of a human arm amid the sharp edges of rubble.

"What's this?" the middle-aged worker exclaimed. His eyes widened.

The older man asked, "Is it a body?"

"Yes, a woman. The worker knelt down to analyze the naked woman.

"Yeah, she's a *laowai*."

"Indeed, look at her fair complexion."

"Why is she here?"

"She must be a prostitute?"

"From Kazakhstan?"

"Maybe, she looks foreign yet Asiatic."

The younger laborer nodded and suggested, "She could be Russian."

"Is she alive?" The older migrant worker's hands trembled and his forehead furrowed.

The younger worker shook his head. "I don't think so." He leaned closer to observe her more carefully and analyzed her wrist, searching for a pulse. "She's not breathing. Look at the bruises, laceration, and burn marks."

The older man nodded with disgust. "Rich people and their perversions."

"And they look down on us!"

"Some things never change," lamented the older man who had survived the Cultural Revolution, the Great Leap Forward, and extreme poverty.

"What should we do with her body?" asked the younger man.

"Add it to the pile for burning," the old man responded with a heavy sigh.

CHAPTER 4
Lana Hayaak

I felt incredibly drowsy, almost paralyzed, and my head ached. My mouth was dry and I was incredibly thirsty.

It was as if I had been asleep for days. I could barely open my eyes or even breathe. The air was scorching hot and thin. I wondered where I was as I laid on my back, desperately trying to wake. I could smell a crude combination of rotting flesh, sewage, and smoke.

I was in pain. My body was cut up, and my bruised legs throbbed. I felt sharp objects piercing my shoulder, which caused me to flinch. I bit my dry lips until I could taste my own blood.

I surmised that I was lying on a mountain of trash. When I finally opened my eyes, I realized I was indeed spread out on top of a heap of garbage covered in layers of filth.

My body was completely bare. I was without even a stitch of clothing. Humiliation oozed through my veins. I wondered which was worse, the drying blood across my aching limbs or the shame of my predicament.

My flesh felt tender and damaged like I was melting.

Something ran and prickled against my chest. I peeked down and saw an army of insects congregating on my naked breasts now covered with a rash of red wounds.

My toes started to burn, and I could no longer hold back because the pain was excruciating. I started screaming at the top of my lungs and wouldn't stop. I was in an oven surrounded by trash and was being cremated alive.

CHAPTER 5

A woman was screaming at the top of her lungs.

The migrant workers dropped their shovels. They stared at one another and gasped while their dark eyes widened with alarm.

"Hey, did you hear that?"

"Yes!"

The men ran to the oven, their mouths gaping open in shock. Looks of horror flickered across their fatigued faces.

"She's alive!"

"Quick, do something!"

"What?"

"Hurry, get her out of there!"

The workers dove toward the oven, coughing from the toxic smoke. They reached for the woman's soot covered arms and pulled her slender, pale body out onto the ground. They threw old, dirty blankets on her frame and stamped out the fire, before dragging her to an open field. Lying listlessly, she passed out.

"Burned alive," the younger worker observed.

"Yeah," the old man agreed.

"What do we do?"

"Take her to the hospital!"

PART 3

CHAPTER 1
Shanghai, China — 2017
Daniel Petersen

The police detective was right. It was time for me to get the hell out of Shanghai. I guess he was tired of my inquiries regarding Lana Hayaak, whom I met in 2009. She abruptly left Shanghai. But then six years later, her husband, a pharmaceutical executive hired me to tail her before mysteriously disappearing.

Most of the expats had left, making it difficult for me to get PI work. After all, most of my gigs involved following married men. So now my Batman, the pet name I'd given to Lana because she reminded me of my favorite childhood superhero, was more than just an expired case. She was an obsession.

I sat at an old desk by the window of my studio apartment in the *Hong Qiao* district. I fiddled around with my computer because my Internet connection was lousy. Just as it started to work, I got a call from Mom via Skype. It was midnight in China, but morning in the States.

"Daniel, can you hear me?"

"Yeah, Mom, how are you?"

"I'm good. I miss you. When are you coming home?"

"Soon, my visa is about to expire."

"That's wonderful. I can't wait for you to get home to Boston."

"Yeah, but flights are expensive now."

"No problem, Daniel. I'll pay for it."

"Not a good time. It's high season."

Mom was a retired school teacher and lived on a fixed income.

"Then what'll you do?" she asked in a shrill tone.

"I'll swing down to Hong Kong."

"Hong Kong is also expensive."

"Yeah, but I can stay with a friend. Plus, I've got a lead to follow-up on."

"What lead? Daniel, are you still obsessing over *that* woman?"

"No, Mom."

My mom let out a high-pitched wail. "Daniel, she's married!"

"She's probably dead," I retorted.

"When are you going to find a nice Jewish girl?"

"Mom, I live in China, not exactly the place to meet Jewish women."

"Come home. I know this lovely girl."

"Mom …"

"Her name is Esther, and she has the most amazing personality."

"Mom, this Internet connection is spotty."

"What was that?"

"Hey, I think we got disconnected."

I slammed my laptop shut. Suddenly Mom's voice was gone, but it wasn't exactly quiet.

I could hear neighbor doors slamming and yelling from the street below my window. It sounded like people were fighting, but in fact it was an ordinary conversation about where to park a bike.

CHAPTER 2

A few weeks later, I'd run out of money because my clients hadn't paid me in months. It was hard enough getting work as a private investigator, but collecting was always a hassle.

To save cash, I avoided taking a taxi or even the bullet train. Instead, I caught the subway and took it from *People's Square* all the way to *Pudong International Airport.*

Lucky me, I sat next to a crying baby during the flight. When we landed, there was heavy traffic on the tarmac. By the time I got through immigration, it was the middle of the night.

Thankfully, Hong Kong is a city that never sleeps. The money changers were wide awake and tersely exchanged my red notes for HK dollars.

I then grabbed the airport train and took it to *Tsing Yi,* an urban island that attracted mainland tourist intent on visiting Disneyland.

***

It was past noon when I finally woke. I could hear the *Ayis* cackling in Cantonese while slamming carts through the narrow, open-air hallways. I sniffed the musky air and could detect the pervasive odor of cigarette smoke as it permeated the room.

I climbed out of my tiny bed and heated water for *Oolong* tea. While passing a beveled mirror, I observed my appearance. I liked my scruffy beard and greasy, overgrown dark curls because I felt it made me look older and more masculine.

I glanced out my hotel window and saw delivery trucks barrel down the crammed highway. By the harbor, freight was unloaded from giant ships marked with Chinese lettering. In the distance, the ocean was calm and greenish brown. Overcast clouds lingered, suggesting future showers which were typical in this region.

I didn't have much to do, and the Internet connection in my room was spotty because I was on a high floor. Thus, I headed downstairs to the lobby. Soon, I was soaking in sweat. Hong Kong's humidity was a sharp contrast to Shanghai.

Sifting through emails on a glass table in the corner, I could hear groups of tourists yelling. A young woman talked loudly to her kids on Skype.

Great, I thought sarcastically.

It was impossible to focus or get any work done with the racket. Plus, I was hungry, so I wandered to a restaurant in the basement. Under a spotlight of fluorescent lights, I walked past rows of cement stalls where cooks tossed fresh vegetables, noodles, and condiments in their woks. Steam billowed into voluminous cloudy layers. Smoke emanated into the halls and created stains on an otherwise sterile ceiling.

The crowded hall consisted of folks bantering in Cantonese. Shifty eyes occasionally glanced in my direction, which was typical. Being the only white guy in the room was something I was used to and didn't mind since I didn't get enough attention as a kid.

I wasn't in the mood for authentic cuisine such as dumplings or noodle soup. So, I headed outside into the street and entered a convenience store where I bought a package of processed meat made from the lowest quality of animal parts.

As I sat down on the rough pavement of the corner of a sidewalk, a slender black cat inched her way up to me and meowed coyly. I peered into her luminous green eyes which implored me for scraps. I ripped off the plastic of my sausage and offered her a nibble. The feline sniffed indignantly, tossed her pink nose in the air, and took off.

"Ha," I yelled, "this sausage isn't good enough for you? You remind me of Lana."

Batman was super fussy about her diet and rarely ate anything that didn't come from the soil. Maybe that's why she looked the same in 2016 as she did when we first met in 2009. In those years, I'd packed on over fifty pounds and grown a beard. I guess I should care more about my appearance, but I was no Aaron Walker. I reeled babes in with my witty lines and effervescent personality.

When I finished eating, I returned upstairs and exited the modest hotel through glass doors. I had to convince the shuttle driver that I was a guest because he assumed, I was a vagabond attempting to hitch a ride. Eventually, after numerous phone calls by the concierge, the staff agreed to take me to the subway station.

It was time for me to head to the center of Hong Kong.

CHAPTER 3
Daniel Petersen

Sitting on the crowded metro headed to Central, I observed children sitting quietly. No one stepped on me or pointed fingers. If they caught my eye, they politely smiled. I checked my phone and realized Mom had called.

I loved Mom, but her attempts at matchmaking were overbearing. She wanted me to find a nice Jewish girl, but it's not as if Dad had been a nice Jewish boy.

My grandparents fled Russia after World War II, but through hard work managed to save a lot to provide my mother with a relatively privileged life. She attended an Ivy League school and dated politicians. Unfortunately, she partied too much. Mom blew through most of her trust fund by the time I was twelve.

I never knew my biological dad. Apparently, he was someone Mom briefly dated before marrying my stepdad, Ned Petersen.

I figured Ned was partly to blame for Mom's money problems. He liked throwing it around. I would wake during their fights and hear her screaming, "If you don't grow up, I'm taking Daniel to Israel —— we'll live in a kibbutz!"

Ned wasn't Jewish. That was another source of conflict. Anyway, one day, I came home and the only dad I'd ever known was gone.

***

When we got to my stop, I pushed through thick crowds and jumped out of the subway. I was now in *Wan Chai*, a district famous for its bars and clubs. It's an excellent place to grab a drink, enjoy a live band, or to find a new "friend" for the night.

Wan Chai had been drastically cleaned up in recent years. However, thanks to Richard Mason's 1957 novel *The World of Suzie Wong*, it retained a stained reputation.

It was Friday night, and I was confident that I'd see Aaron Walker.

While walking, I thought about the last time Lana and I talked:

Flashback — 2015

After the office party, I followed her to the subway station where she struggled with the ticket machine. I confronted her and said, "You're into Walker, aren't you?"

She ignored me, so I blurted, "What? No denial?"

Lana finally turned to face me and coldly replied, "Why would I deny something so plainly true?"

Angrily, I snapped, "I thought you were different from other women."

"Good God, why would you think that?"

"Dunno," I stammered.

She brushed past me and quickly headed for the train. I pursued her and shouted, "You only like men if they have money or a hot body."

Lana froze, turned, and furiously took steps in my direction.

Nervously I walked backward, but exclaimed, "Why not give a nice guy a chance?"

Like a panther, she stalked up to me and growled, "Because you're not a nice guy."

"Yeah, I am."

"You're just another manipulative misogynist in a clown's suit."

"Hey, I'm debonair," I asserted while adjusting my top hat, a favorite clothing item.

She hissed, "Guess what Petersen —"

"I'm listening."

"Women like men who love women. It's that simple."

"I love women."

"No, you don't."

"Hey, I'm a good son and a great guy."

"I don't give a damn. Just get the hell out of my way."

"You're hot when you're fired up."

"Jerk," Lana muttered under her breath.

I chased after her and yelled, "I like a strong woman, but you're too much. You're a bulldozer."

She spun around while walking and shouted, "And how is that my problem?"

I paused, took a deep breath, and in a boyish tone explained, "You're all about image."

Lana's body stiffened. I continued, "Women like you are in love with ideas and not reality."

She tilted her head quizzically and stood still as if waiting for me to finish.

So I said, "You're the type of girl who grew up liking fictional characters in books, men who say the right things because women writers created them. No guy ever met your standards. You went for Steiger because he fit your criteria on paper, but he's a control freak, and you're not in love with him.

Now you're infatuated with Walker because he doesn't say much, so you project what you want, but if you actually got to know him, you'd discover he's just like any other guy which is exactly what you don't want."

For once, Batman had nothing to say. She hesitated for a moment before walking away.

The woman befuddled me. It was obvious she wanted me, so why didn't she just say so?

CHAPTER 4
2016
Lana Hayaak

I have no idea how long I'd been asleep for, but as I struggled to open my eyes, I confronted complete darkness. My vision eventually became accustomed to the dark, and I realized I was in a hospital, lying on a bed with clean white sheets. I wondered where I was. With considerable effort, I attempted to get up. I fell and knocked over a table. The crashing sound of metal hitting the tile ricocheted through my head.

The door swung wide open, and light poured in. I winced. Lithe nurses dressed in crisp uniforms raced into the room with alarm. They flicked on fluorescent lights that overwhelmed me. I felt dizzy. Surprisingly, the slender nurses were able to carefully place me back into bed.

In Mandarin, they whispered, "She's finally awake."

"Indeed, should we get the doctor?"

"No, it's too late. His shift is over. Let's put Miss back to sleep."

"Good idea. The doctor can see her in the morning."

I felt like a prisoner trapped in my bed. I wanted to sit

upright and tried desperately to do so, but the nurses immediately forced me down. My attempts to resist with what little strength I had were met with a sharp needle prick in the tender part of my arm. Soon, I faded away and entered a world that was dreamy and tranquil, and unlike my current world.

***

I felt groggy, yet wide awake — if that makes any sense. Lying in a fetal position, I hugged my pillow. As I fluttered my eyes open, I noticed hopeful rays of warmth peeking through the thick curtains in an otherwise sterile, desolate room.

Though dim, I could discern a young man wearing a white lab coat. He stood at my bedside. I jolted alert and tried to articulate a myriad of ideas that cluttered my mind. Thoughts raced through my head like an army of kittens parading across the clouds in heaven. I had so much to say and didn't know where to begin.

However, the man, whom I presumed to be a doctor, gently placed his index finger over his lips, and whispered, "Careful, please take it easy."

"The cat's name is Dinah," I stammered anxiously.

The man nodded but said nothing.

We stared at one another for a few minutes. I analyzed his dark eyes and wondered if I'd seen them before. They looked familiar.

Finally, I tilted my head to the side and in a childish tone asked, "Doctor, where am I?"

"Outside of Beijing."

"Oh, I see," I replied. I wondered if I had been here before. The place felt familiar.

"What's your name?"

The racing thoughts suddenly disappeared, leaving me speechless. I felt extremely stressed by this challenging question. What was my name? I felt an incredibly sharp pain in my forehead.

Finally, I replied indignantly, "Doctor, the cat's name is Dinah."

"I know," he replied. "But what's your name?

I continued to stare at him, but then looked away because I felt frustrated. I fought to contain myself and resisted the urge to pout. Instead, I bit my lip.

The doctor nodded calmly as if he half expected this response. "Do you remember anything?"

The throbbing sensation in my forehead persisted. "I don't know," I whispered.

"I see," the doctor responded. "Please take it easy. You were badly injured. You suffered first degree burns on your legs. Your head took many beatings. You're lucky to be alive."

"What?" I exclaimed. The doctor's information made little sense. Why on earth would that happen?

"Miss, you were left for dead."

What the doctor said was absurd. I was tired, so I fell back in bed and decided to take a nap.

CHAPTER 5
Beijing — 2016

A government official sat behind his desk in a dimly lit office adorned with books. The man was in his late sixties but looked younger. An agent took a seat and spoke deferentially.

"Sir, I recently communicated with the doctor."

The official nodded.

"The foreign woman who was almost cremated alive has finally woken."

"I see."

"What should we do?"

The official leaned back in his chair, thought for a moment, then replied, "We must avoid letting this get public."

"Yes, we've kept her in a remote, isolated facility. No one but the nurses, doctors, and some laborers know about this woman."

"Good, and make sure it stays that way because if this story gets out, it will cause so much embarrassment."

"But we have technically done nothing wrong," the agent protested.

"Doesn't matter; you know how the world looks at China."

"She *is* responsible for thousands of deaths."

"We don't know that for sure."

"The people who tortured her thought so."

The older man shrugged and reached for his cup of tea. "Maybe, maybe not."

"For certain, China is in no way responsible for this woman's condition."

The official nodded. "Yes, I know, but it doesn't matter."

"Then this would be a public embarrassment."

"Have you talked to her yet? She could have valuable information."

The agent shook his head. "She speaks like a child. The doctor insists she's suffered irreparable brain damage."

"Then she's useless."

"What should we do with her?"

"Deliver medical supplies to one of our allies. They desperately need vaccines due to an embargo. Then leave her under their care."

"But what will they do with her?"

"I'm not sure, but she'll be much safer anywhere but here."

"I agree with you, Sir. After all, the people who tortured and tried to kill her will return if they find out she's still alive."

"Yes, and it's only a matter of time before someone gets sloppy and leaks information to the media. So hurry. You have very little time."

"Yes, Sir, we'll take care of this immediately."

The older man leaned back in his chair and murmured repeatedly, "*di diao, di diao,*" which means to keep a low profile in Mandarin. It's something Chinese managers frequently say.

CHAPTER 6
Hong Kong — 2017
Daniel Petersen

Aaron Walker was at a sports bar with his friends while girls buzzed nearby. Guys like Walker had it so easy. Tall and athletic, he had clearly won the genetic lottery. Asia has plenty of Eurasians, probably because Hong Kong attracts foreigners from all over the world. There were gorgeous Russian and Eastern European models working at most clubs and bars.

However, Aaron and Lana were distinct from other mixes. Aaron was taller. He was about 6'4" and had a stronger, square jaw. In contrast, Lana had exceptionally delicate features, high cheekbones, porcelain white skin, and a pointed nose. Both possessed ambiguous qualities.

It was noisy as I stumbled forward and shouted, "Hey, remember me?"

"Huh?" Aaron exclaimed with confusion.

"Two years ago. Shanghai."

"Not really," Aaron replied. He took a sip of beer and whispered something into the ear of a skinny girl wearing a short, tight dress.

"Remember Lana?"

Aaron released the girl he had been holding, turned to me, and asked, "Why?"

"I know what happened to her," I lied.

***

Aaron and I sat in a booth at a dark, damp dive bar drinking imported beer. It was past 3 a.m., and only the sad stragglers remained. A couple of older men played a game of pool while bored ladies of the night lingered in the corners. They had weathered expressions on their faces. The bartender looked irritable as he wiped down the counter and rifled through cash in the register.

"So what's your deal?" Aaron demanded.

"Huh?"

"Why are you still investigating Hayaak?"

"I'm not."

"Then why are you here?"

"I had to renew my visa."

"I don't mean — why are you in Hong Kong? Why are you *here* with me?"

"Don't you want to know what happened to her?"

"Not really," Aaron replied.

"Why not?"

"Lana meant nothing to me."

I paused and took a sip of what was now warm beer. "Yeah, you've got a point."

Aaron stared back and crossed his arms.

I continued, "Why do I care about this bird? It's not like Lana ever cared about me."

"How did you meet?" Aaron suddenly asked.

"I thought you didn't care about her," I reminded him.

"I don't," he snapped. "I'm trying to figure you out."

"We met on a flight in 2009. She was new in Shanghai and didn't know anyone. So we hung out a few times."

Flashback — Shanghai, 2009

It was a Saturday afternoon in mid-July. Lana wore a pencil skirt, a black blouse, and high heels. We were at a Parisian-style café in the French Concession. I took all my dates there because chicks loved the décor: black and white marble floors, Casablanca fans, and dark wood paneling. Baroque pictures covered the walls and gaudy pastries filled glass cases in the front room. We were at a table in the back hidden by red velvet drapes which I chose to get Lana in the mood.

"My stepdad had it rough," I lamented.

"How so?" Lana asked while sipping a cappuccino.

"He caught his first wife in bed with another man. Meanwhile, my mom was cheating on him."

By sharing a personal story of my own, I hoped Lana would confide in me. We'd connect, form an imaginary bond and wind up back at my place.

Instead, Lana said tersely, "I see," while carefully placing her cup back on the saucer.

"Yeah, so it really sucks being a dude in today's world," I continued.

"Right, because women were put on this planet to serve your every waking demand?" Lana asked with hostility in her voice.

This wasn't going the way I planned. However, I could sense tension which is always good. The worst thing is a woman's indifference. If I got that vibe, I'd make a back-handed compliment to illicit an emotional reaction which I could always shift in my favor.

"Well, no, but chicks need to be loyal," I stated matter-of-factly. I postured to seem more manly. I needed to dominate Batman and put her in her place.

Lana glared at me.

I stared back but had trouble holding my gaze the way I do with most girls. Instead, I studied Lana's face like it was one of the prints on the wall. It was a seduction technique designed to flatter women into submission.

"After my girlfriend dumped me, Megan slept with so many other guys."

"Yeah, how dare she?" Lana quipped sarcastically. "I mean; you own her right?"

"Whoa, I didn't peg you for a feminist."

"I'm a realist."

"I'm real," I said with confusion.

"Petersen, you're about as genuine as cubic zirconia."

"I don't think we gel well," I quipped. Usually, when I told girls that our personalities weren't compatible, they'd fall for the bait and then argue why we're meant to be together.

Instead, Lana gave me an icy look and said, "You've got a talent for pointing out the obvious."

"Huh?"

"I only connect with people who share my intellect," she said in a frosty tone.

"Whoa, you're an elitist," I said shaking my finger at her. So high and mighty, I thought angrily.

"Quit labeling me."

I stammered while trying to think of a witty comeback.

Lana leaned forward and hissed, "I've been aware of your tactics from day one."

"Like what?" I asked feigning innocence.

"Whenever men discuss their feelings immediately, I raise an eyebrow."

"Me, too," I said attempting to seem empathetic. Then I tried a different ploy. This lioness was a hard kitten to tame. So I leaned back, tilted my head to the side, and asked, "How can a mere mortal like myself appeal to a queen like you?"

Lana groaned. "Share facts, problem-solve, and offer a concise analysis."

I was surprised because this wasn't the response I expected. Batman was way out of my league, and I was intrigued, so I asked, "Why've you been seeing me, anyway?"

I hoped that by playing possum I'd make her lose her guard.

"I've been studying you," she responded while eyeing me

skeptically.

"Oh, yeah," I said with a big grin. "Well, you can study more of me back at my place."

Lana stood up, tossed cash on the table, and headed for the door.

I chased after her. She stopped, spun around, and declared, "Conversations with you are consistently unchallenging and inappropriate."

"Okay, okay," I ordered. "Calm down."

"No, don't tell me to calm down!"

"Geez, Batman. You need to chill out," I yelled as she stormed off with her nose in the air. "You've clearly got anger management issues. I think you're suffering from an impairment."

Lana stopped walking, pivoted and said, "The person who has a deficit is you."

"Huh?" I asked with interest. She was staring into my eyes, and it's like she could see right into my soul.

Lana pointed at my chest and said, "You're the one with issues which is why you try your dime-store pseudo-science nonsense with women."

"Hey, I took an expensive course," I protested.

"You should get your money back."

"Not likely," I said dryly. In my experience, my techniques worked, but it was a numbers game and all about an unhappy woman in the wrong place at the right time.

Lana shook her head and declared, "Petersen, it's bad enough that we live in a world where we're told what to do and what to think."

"Yeah, but you're going to be a lawyer," I replied envying the fact that she'd have autonomy over her life.

She continued, "But forcing people to feel is beyond overbearing."

I was speechless. Maybe that was my problem. Growing up, my hysterical Mom drove me crazy because she was always trying to make me understand how she and other women felt. I didn't care. Mom was an emotional time bomb waiting to explode. Her analysis of the female psyche never made me sensitive to women's issues. It only made me resentful.

Why didn't anyone care about my issues? Maybe this was why I was in China, surrounded by foreign girls who didn't speak English. I liked women who didn't share their problems with me.

I fantasized about being a nobleman in ancient China because those guys had it easy. Nowadays, Chinese girls were as demanding as the ones back home. Here in Shanghai, the princesses were the worst, making men carry their purses for them. I contemplated relocating to South East Asia where women kept their hair and skirts long, but their opinions to themselves.

Batman was different. She knew when I was feigning empathy and couldn't be manipulated, yet she was feminine while fighting back. It was clear she hungered for me. Her denials were hilarious.

So I joked, "Baby, you can force me to do anything."

Lana's eyes widened with alarm, she grabbed her purse and took off running, which was amusing since she was wearing high heels.

Aaron listened, raised his right eyebrow, and said, "Yeah sounds about right. So why are you hung up on her?"

"Nah, it's not like that," I protested.

Aaron glared at me.

"Are you religious?" I asked.

"Not really."

"But growing up, you went to church, right?"

"Dad's relatives are hardcore Baptists, so yeah, I know all about organized religion."

I nodded. "Okay, so remember the story about *David and Bathsheba?*"

"Not really," Aaron responded with a wide yawn. He glanced first at his watch, then at the door, evidently wondering what had happened to the women.

I continued, "One day King David looked out his window and saw this voluptuous woman bathing. He was very attracted to her. The problem was that she was *already* married."

"So, you think you're King David or something? Didn't he kill Goliath?"

"You said you didn't know the Bible," I reminded

Aaron.

"This has nothing to do with the Bible," he replied while shaking his head.

"Oh, yeah."

"And this has nothing to do with Lana."

"Yeah, it's about justice," I countered. "I'm a private investigator and won't rest until this crime is solved."

"Nah, Petersen, this is all about *you*."

CHAPTER 7

It was past 4 a.m. The bar consisted of leftovers, desperately crawling around like dying flies, searching for company. The manager had flipped on disco lights that cast neon rainbow shadows across the room which smelled of alcohol, cigarettes, and sweat. Overweight men in their fifties struggled to stand upright while women in short faux leather skirts acted as crutches.

I slurred, "What?"

Aaron replied, "You're a fantasist."

"Come again?"

"How are you like King David?"

"Okay," I conceded, "Maybe Paris and Helen of Troy would be a better analogy. Steiger is Menelaus."

Aaron shook his head. "Keep telling yourself that."

Suddenly I blurted, "Lana was a sadist."

"I never got that impression," Aaron replied calmly.

"Yeah, that's because she liked you."

Aaron shrugged. "Never try to dominate her type."

"Huh?"

"You've got to let women like Lana chase you."

"I tried," I said with an exacerbated sigh.

Aaron grinned. "It's about confidence. You've either got it or you don't. Women smell it a mile away."

I groaned. This wasn't what I wanted to hear.

"You're like a lot of women I know," Aaron continued.

"I doubt it," I snapped.

"What was your dad like?"

I was suddenly taken aback by Aaron's interest and relaxed a bit. I quickly came up with an elaborate lie, "Um, Dad was a Mossad agent killed in the field."

This wasn't the response Aaron expected because he exclaimed, "Your dad was Israeli? How was he killed?"

I struggled for an answer, and carefully lied, "Mom met Dad while studying in a Kibbutz. Grandma survived the pogroms, but Dad couldn't survive a secret mission in Afghanistan to take out the Ruskies."

Aaron nodded respectfully. "That's awesome. I studied Krav Maga."

I was worried. I'd pegged Aaron as a student of an Asian form of self-defense like Tae Kwon Do or Karate. I sure as hell didn't know Israel's renowned martial arts, Krav Maga, so I quipped, "I'm more of a lover and not a fighter."

Thankfully, Aaron changed the subject. "You're broke aren't you?"

"Are you psychic or something?"

"Nope, I'm observant. You've got broke plastered across your forehead."

"So do you," I joked.

Aaron stopped drinking. His face was tense. "Yeah, I do. My dad got pancreatic cancer, and his hospital bills are mounting."

I nodded but felt slightly guilty about my joke.

"I'm in Hong Kong searching for investors," Aaron continued. He paused and took a swig of beer.

"What about your factories in Guangzhou?"

Aaron nodded. "We've still got a few outsourcing contracts, but I need more capital to buy newer equipment and acquire more projects."

I looked doubtful as I responded, "New projects?"

"I want to expand into a different technology, but stuff that requires heavy funding."

I shrugged since this wasn't my area.

Aaron asked, "You know who has plenty of money, right?"

"Everyone else."

"Steiger," Aaron clarified.

"Sure," I agreed. "Curt's got a ton of money, but he's in Silicon Valley."

"Yeah, so I was thinking —"

I shook my head. "No way, Steiger fired me, and he hates your guts."

"Sure, but there's one thing Steiger loves."

"Lana," I replied.

"Asian women," Aaron corrected me.

"So?"

"I've got this sister."

"Does she look like you?" I joked.

Aaron shook his head, leaned back, and replied, "Trinity looks like Lana."

I raised an eyebrow.

Aaron pulled out his phone and handed it to me. I stared at the picture. "She looks nothing like Lana."

Aaron shrugged. "Trinity is mixed like Lana."

"So what, they still look nothing alike."

Aaron nodded and glanced at his watch.

I continued, "What's your plan? Fix Trinity up with Steiger so she can get his money? Bad idea, that's like the time I went to summer camp. My pet goldfish Goldie died, and Mom replaced it with an angelfish, as if I wouldn't know the difference."

Aaron stared at me. "Man, you've got serious issues."

I didn't say anything.

Aaron continued, "I thought you'd polish Trinity up and

have her pitch Steiger for the capital I need."

I pondered this idea while examining the photo and stammered, "Are … are those real?"

Aaron leaned over and smacked me. "Hey, that's my sister."

"Ouch," I squealed. "Yeah, Trinity is a good-looking woman."

"Thanks," Aaron agreed.

Silently I noted that Trinity was attractive. She was very slender with augmented breasts, coarse curly dark hair, big brown eyes, and full sensual lips. However, her skin looked worn from too much sun, smoking, and alcohol. She wore pastel lipstick, blue eye-shadow, and a leopard-patterned tight dress that was low cut and revealed cleavage.

"I thought you could coach Trinity to be more like Lana," Aaron suggested.

"How?" I asked incredulously.

"You're smart."

"Sure, I was a Classics major."

"Yeah, see. You know all that Greek history stuff."

"Yes, but I'm no Pygmalion."

"But you could be," Aaron suggested.

"You're familiar with that play?"

"Yeah, I've read mythology." Changing the subject, Aaron said, "I'll pay your way —"

"Why?" I was amazed. Why would a guy like Aaron pay my way back to the U.S.? Was he trying to pay me off? Bribe me to forget about Lana's killer?

"A deal with Steiger is huge, and I need your help with that."

"I'll do my best, but Curt isn't an easy guy."

Aaron nodded. "Yep, plus Trinity is in a bad place. You seem like a good guy."

"I wish Lana had thought that."

"C'mon Petersen, that woman was impossible to please. Unlike Lana, my sister would kill for a guy like you."

"Yeah, Lana was so high and mighty," I complained.

"Yeah, but you're still fixated on her. You need a new project."

"Okay, but first you need to tell me what happened with Lana."

Aaron sipped his beer casually and replied, "Nothing."

I was very drunk and blurted, "Did you kill her?"

Aaron leaned forward and said smoothly, "Ah, so the truth comes out."

"Huh."

He sat upright, narrowed his eyes, and steepled his hands. An awkward silence developed. I focused on a vein bulging from his forehead while he clenched his jaw and fists.

"This is why you're here? You think I killed Lana?"

"Originally, I thought it was Steiger because he had the motive."

"Absolutely," Aaron agreed. "Steiger stood to make $25 million which he'd have to split with his wife who was bound to leave him."

"How did you know?"

"Lana told me."

"Yeah, you were the last person to see her."

"Yep, on the train, so why do you think I killed her?"

"Her disappearance was sloppy. That's not Steiger's style."

Aaron stared at me. "If I'm her killer, aren't you afraid of me?"

"Not really," I lied. "There are CCTV cameras everywhere."

I pulled out a photocopy of Lana's diary.

Aaron snatched it, and while scrutinizing pages demanded, "Why's this covered in beer stains?"

"Um, long story," I replied sheepishly.

Impatiently, Aaron scanned the diary and exclaimed irritably, "Lana's story is off."

"So what happened?"

Aaron took a deep breath and said, "I was at a club, entertaining clients at the back of the second floor."

Flashback — Shanghai, August 2009

Around midnight, I heard shouting from downstairs. I jumped up and went over to the railing. Everyone was staring at a woman dancing on the stage. She had porcelain white skin and classical features. It wasn't just that she was pretty. It was the flicker of passion in her eyes. She was so ethereal.

I thought she saw me, but then a couple of women pulled her into their group.

I wanted to ask her to dance, but my investors insisted on leaving. On the way out, I asked the security guard about her.

"Ah, that's Lana, just another student. Come back tomorrow," Jacov suggested.

I returned the next day and the manager joined me for a drink. As I was telling Paul about work, I looked up and saw Lana enter.

It was raining outside, but her cheeks were red and she had a radiant glow.

"Who's she?" I asked.

Paul sneered. "That's Lana. She works at a local firm."

"Is she Asian?" I couldn't help asking. After all, she could almost pass for white. Or was she mixed like me?

"I don't know. Lana is Lana," Paul replied irritably.

I nodded. "Can you introduce us?"

"Yeah, but careful man, she's a real bitch."

"Cool, I like a challenge."

Paul snorted. "There's always been tension between me and Lana."

"Oh, yeah?" I asked to be polite, but frankly, I didn't care about this guy's problems.

"Women do not argue with me."

I shrugged. "Yeah, well this is China."

"Usually women get flustered and nervous."

"Because they're intimidated by you," I joked with a chuckle.

Paul took me seriously and began a monologue, "Yeah, exactly. Women want to do a lot of things with me, but this one just wants to talk. At first, it was exciting, but now it's tiresome. Her attitude and opinions piss me off. I've tried to rattle her with personal insults, and she looks at me without any fear. She doesn't respect me!"

"I'll put her in her place," I promised.

Paul looked doubtful, but then said, "Give me a second."

He ran up to Lana who was standing alone by the railing checking texts. At first, the two interacted like old friends. But soon the smile vanished from Lana's _face_. She looked ready to slap Paul, so I approached.

I heard Paul joke, "At least prostitution is more honest than your chosen profession."

Lana snapped, "You don't belong in customer service."

"Oh, yeah, well you don't belong in a bar if you can't take a joke," the manager retorted. But he suddenly noticed me standing in front of them and said, "Aaron, meet Lana. Lana, this is Aaron."

I heard him whisper loudly into her ear, "Be nice."

As Paul walked past me, he muttered, "Good luck man, you'll need it."

Lana's feathers were ruffled but did her best to hide it as she greeted me politely by shaking my hand. She smiled, but it's like she was looking through me as opposed to at me.

"Can I buy you a drink?" I asked.

She clasped her glass. "Thanks, but I already have one."

"Paul tells me you're a paralegal?"

Lana shook her head and looked away. "I'm a law student. And you?"

"I run outsourcing factories in Guangzhou."

Lana nodded. "So you're in Shanghai for the weekend?"

"Yeah, tomorrow I'm going to Beijing to meet an investor."

Lana's face grew concerned as she suddenly looked at me, and said, "Oh, do be careful."

"Excuse me?"

"Those taxi drivers in Beijing are ruthless. I hope they won't take advantage of you."

"Are you serious?" I demanded. Was she blind?

"Those guys can be quite savage."

I shook my head and said firmly, "I can handle them."

"Of course, you can."

I still wanted to know her ethnicity, so I asked, "Do you speak Chinese?"

Lana laughed and in a haughty tone replied, "That's more subtle than your earlier question."

"Huh?" I was confused.

"Didn't you ask Paul if I'm Asian?"

"Yes," I replied, but wondered why Paul shared my inquiry.

"Well, that wasn't a very original question."

Geez, Paul was right, I thought. This woman was a pain. I wanted to say, why are you racist? Instead, I said, "I'm mixed. My Dad is American and my mother is Japanese."

I hoped she'd relate to me.

Instead, Lana lashed out with, "My grandmother barely survived a Japanese concentration camp."

This wasn't the reaction I wanted.

She abruptly pulled away, so I confronted her and said, "Hey, that's not fair. My family had nothing to do with that. They were in internment camps."

Lana suddenly stopped, reflected for a moment and remarked, "Japanese people care about animals."

"Animals?" I asked.

"I'm vegan."

"Oh, brother," I said with disgust.

"Because I don't condone killing."

"Where I'm from hunting is a way of life."

I expected Lana to pull away again, but instead, she asked, "Where are you from?"

This chick was complicated. Her swift mood change from hostile to curious indicated that our exchange wasn't genuine. She was doing what a lot of women do to guys; testing me to see how I'd respond to an insult. It was her way of determining whether I was strong enough to stand up to her, but safe enough to hang out with. And clearly, I'd won this round.

"Michigan. And you?"

"San Francisco."

"I've never been there, but I've always wanted to visit."

Lana smiled but looked away to read messages on her phone. I studied her face carefully while she explained, "My friends keep texting. I was supposed to be across town tonight, but due to traffic ended up here."

I joked, "So we almost didn't meet?"

It was a line I'd heard my Dad's buddies use at bars.

She blushed and replied, "My friends want to go to karaoke."

I laughed, stared into her eyes, and asked, "So do you want to go to KTV or do you want to stay here with me?"

Her cheeks flamed as she nervously confessed, "I want to dance!"

"Then, let's dance." I took her hand and led her to the empty dance floor where she immediately started dancing.

Lana twirled around and asked flirtatiously, "Have you ever had a Eurasian girlfriend?"

I laughed. "No, but I've always wanted one."

I felt uncomfortable so I headed to the bar and asked, "Do you want some shots?"

"Um, sure," Lana agreed reluctantly. She joined me, but fumbled with the lime while sipping the tequila. She had no idea what she was doing.

"You're supposed to drink it in one shot," I explained.

Lana nodded, but still sipped the tequila.

"Last night was so much more fun," she said girlishly.

"Yeah, I was here with a big group."

"You were?"

"Upstairs, in the back," I replied. "Hey, what time did you leave?"

"Um, 3 a.m.," she replied with sudden unease.

I wanted to ask if she'd left alone, but her arms were now crossed as she took a step backward. The shots hadn't loosened her up.

I sensed her distrust and worried she'd leave, so I asked, "Do you want to go someplace else?"

Lana looked at her phone and said, "My friends are at a nearby club."

I nodded figuring this would be goodbye.

She started to walk away, but then stopped, pivoted and asked, "Aaron, do you want to come?"

Aaron stopped talking, studied his watch and said, "Hey Petersen, it's late. I need to get home." He motioned for the bartender and paid the entire bill.

"Yeah," I agreed. "I should probably get back to *Tsing Yi.*"

"So what about my sister?" Aaron asked.

"What about the rest of the story?"

"I'll finish during our flight to Houston."

"Our flight?"

"Yeah, call me later," Aaron said as he scribbled down his number and left the bar. The sun was rising and locals anxiously rushed to work.

CHAPTER 8
Western China — 2016
Lana Hayaak

Weak as a newborn kitten, but desperate to explore the world and breathe fresh air, I happily agreed to the adventure I'd been promised. Apparently, we would soon begin a long journey to the west. I was so excited I could barely contain myself.

Early in the morning as the sun rose, my favorite nurse entered my room and helped me bathe. Fan was ever so gentle while sponging my body, which was starting to heal. She toweled me off and assisted as I slipped into a simple gray dress.

"Where are we going?" I exclaimed with girlish enthusiasm. I felt like a primary student about to embark on her first field trip to the aquarium.

"It's a surprise," Fan responded with a big grin.

"Oh, goody, I love surprises," I said with genuine delight. "I mean; I think I do." My fervent gaiety was suddenly replaced with despair because I had no idea what I liked. I didn't even know who I was. I almost wanted to burst into tears but bit my lips to hold back sorrow.

The room rapidly turned cold and what light had shown through the windows faded. Angry clouds lingered in the sky and thunder erupted. Soon it began to pour, and the wind howled. I shivered as fear replaced happiness. I blinked rapidly and felt incredible pressure in my forehead. A radiating, throbbing pain.

Fan had been quietly watching me, but she now put her hand on my shoulder and whispered, "It's okay Miss."

"Is that my name?" I asked.

***

Fan was a young nurse from Qingdao. She had round eyes, cream-colored skin, and a heart-shaped face that mirrored her compassion. She strolled down a dark, empty hallway with another nurse, Jia, who had copper-colored skin, an oblong-face, and almond-shaped eyes.

It was almost midnight, and the hospital was vacant. There were no receptionists, orderlies, or other patients in the dimly lit yet immaculately clean medical center. It was eerily quiet with no one around. Equally sinister was the absence of the usual din of ringing phones.

Fan remarked, "Our new patient acts like a little girl."

"Yes, but she's over thirty," responded Jia.

"Really? She looks good for her age."

"The dentist examined her teeth. He said she must be over thirty."

"Her skin, even after the burns, is still soft."

"You mean her upper body," Jia corrected her colleague. "Her feet and legs were badly burned. She'll have scars for life."

"Someone must have cared about her a lot," Fan mused.

"Why would you think that?"

"Because she looks good for her age."

Jia shook her head. "Maybe for a time, but such affection didn't last."

"Why?"

"She was tortured quite badly."

"By bad people, maybe her loved ones are searching for her," Fan said hopefully.

"Like who?"

"A husband?"

"Don't be silly," Jia said. "You're such a romantic. If her husband cared about her, we'd hear about it in the news."

"What news? We hardly get anything here."

"Doesn't matter. Someone would know something. Someone would be looking for this patient."

"There's still time."

"Not really," Jia stated firmly, "at least not at this facility."

"If only she'd remember something," Fan remarked.

"Not likely, her mind is like a child which is not uncommon after severe trauma."

"It's unfortunate what will happen to her," Fan lamented with genuine despair.

"There's nothing we can do. Miss won't be our responsibility much longer."

"Yes, with her mind the way it is …"

"She is useless to anyone," Jia opined.

CHAPTER 9
Lana Hayaak

I danced out of the hospital like a sparrow, intent on spreading her wings. I was so giddy that I tripped, fell, and hit my head against the pavement.

Fan and the other nurse rushed to my aide, clutched my upper body, and dragged me up. I heard someone whisper, "Any more blows to the head and she'll be a vegetable."

Moments later, I felt a familiar feeling. It was the prick of a needle in my upper arm. I had become so acquainted with injections that I almost took delight in the sensation. After all, most of the time, I was numb.

When I woke, I felt as if I'd been asleep for days. I struggled to sit upright but kept wobbling. I desperately desired water, but could barely mumble. Fan sitting beside me, became alert, opened a bottle of water, and fed me like an infant. I calmed down.

"Where are we?" I exclaimed while peering out of the van's blackened windows. I stared at endless arid terrain absent of any buildings, people, or life. The land was the color of rust.

"We're almost there," Fan responded.

"But where is there?" I asked like a child.

Fan ignored me, so I drifted back to sleep and dreamt of a city with blue skies, abundant sunlight, and fresh air. There were palm trees, squirrels, and Spanish-style buildings. This dream filled me with a blissful sense of nostalgia. While sleeping, I felt I was at peace somewhere safe.

Hours later, I opened my eyes and realized that the driver was carrying me into a restaurant. I glanced around and realized it was the dead of night. The sky was black but lit with a faint flurry of stars. The land was still dry and dusty. The air was thin but warm. Structures with intricate dome-like features, mosaic tiles, and marble characterized this unique city.

In the distance I observed run-down buildings covered with large, heavily-painted billboards. Men with long gray beards, dark eyes, and black robes stared hauntingly into the streets. They were very proud and with a single look expressed a multitude of words. It was as if they said, "Obey us, or else." However, I had no idea what the signs said because it was in a language I didn't know.

As I sat in a large dining hall, I glanced around with intrigue. The place felt incredibly familiar and yet so foreign.

I sat at a round table with Fan, Jia, and the driver. They ordered several plates of rice, vegetables, and eggplant dishes covered in creamy, fragrant sauces. We also had plenty of tea served in copper pieces.

I was famished. I ate with such intensity that I caught my friends staring. I refer to Fan, Jia, and the driver as my friends because these are the only people I know and may have ever known.

I observed that no one besides my friends conversed in Mandarin. The strangers throughout the room were dressed in long flowing robes and spoke a language that I recognized, but couldn't identify.

I felt trapped in a half-remembered dream that partly resembled a fantasy, but also a horrible nightmare because I was numb. I wondered what was in those syringes Fan had been sticking into my arm. On the one hand, I was tranquil and happy. It was as if I was floating. However, I also felt trapped in quicksand. If I wanted to get up and run away, it'd be impossible. This experience felt like déjà vu as if I'd lived it all before at some other time in my life. I hoped these episodes would trigger actual memories, but my personal history remained a mystery.

After we completed our feast, we ventured to a modest hotel where I remained in the van during the check-in process.

Fan helped me climb into a simple, but clean bed. As I fell into a deep sleep, I was overwhelmed by a false sense of security and a perplexing dream:

I was lying on an ivory-colored sofa in a luxurious apartment decorated with Oriental antiquities. A cat with big green eyes, a red brick nose, and long gray hair sat on my chest purring. I stroked his coat as he gazed at me adoringly. But then a tall irritable man with blonde hair and blue eyes stormed through the door and yelled, "Lana, why is that damned cat on the couch?" My friend instantly jumped off me and scurried out of the living room, his ears back and tail between his legs. I started to protest, but then felt so much anxiety that I woke with alarm.

My body and hair were soaked in sweat. When I opened my eyes, bright rays of the sun shone through the windows. My room was vacant and I felt dehydrated. I stumbled out of bed, put on my shoes, and looked for my nurse.

"Fan," I called. "Fan where are you?"

I ran out of the hotel bedroom into a blast of heat. As I ventured down a dark hallway, I observed plain walls and white tile floors. I was barefoot, so my feet felt cool. There were no windows, so there was little light, except that which emanated from the end of the hallway.

I wandered around shouting Fan's name until I reached

a marble-floored lobby and anxiously approached the front desk. I'm certain that I looked most peculiar standing in public in my sweat-soaked nightgown as I screamed, "Fan! Where is Fan?"

Ceiling fans hummed in the distance while the hotel manager, staff, and guests stared at me. They whispered to one another in their exotic language. But I somehow managed to hear someone say, "I think she's mad."

"Where are the people who were with her?" the front desk manager asked.

"They already checked out," his co-worker replied.

"What?"

"This strange woman's group checked out hours ago and left in the black van that they arrived in."

"But why did they leave her?"

"They had to go to the medical center to deliver vaccines."

"Where am I?" I stammered. "Do you speak English?"

Finally, someone stepped forward and responded in perfect English, "Ma'am, you are in Tehran."

"Tehran?" I repeated with confusion.

"Iran," someone clarified.

I stood mute for an excessive amount of time. I fought to suppress tears. I was so frustrated because I had this weird sensation that I'd been here before or someplace like it. The language, the people, the architecture, and the heat felt oddly familiar. Was *this* home? No, it couldn't be because I didn't feel safe.

It was like I was trapped in limbo and forced to relive the same nightmare over and over again. But I had no idea how or why all of this had started. I didn't know who I was, where I was from, or why I was in Iran.

I felt pierced through my chest as I was overwhelmed by the abandonment, confusion, and stabbing loneliness.

CHAPTER 10
Outside of Tehran, Iran — 2016
Lana

Paradoxically, despite my inability to remember myself, I could recall specific facts. For example, I knew that Iran is famous for its gracious hospitality. That is if you're a guest. I, on the other hand, was a prisoner in this country famous for its rich classical history — Darius the Great, carpets, and long-haired cats.

The hotel didn't know what to do with me, so they called the authorities who escorted me to the police station where I endured hours of interrogation. Unable to answer any questions, the authorities finally decided to deliver me to a new location.

With my hands tied behind my back, I was blindfolded and escorted to a van. I experienced yet another long drive to my new destination.

After a long ride across bumpy roads in unbearable heat, the van jerked to a grinding halt. I flew forward and hit my head against the seat in front of me.

I was grabbed and repositioned by armed guards. I couldn't see but figured out we were walking through narrow halls because we would abruptly turn sharp corners, and I'd bash up against cold, concrete walls. I smelled the faint scent of dampness and sulfur.

Eventually, a guard removed the blindfold. I batted my eyes in the dark and tried to make out a myriad of shadows. As I entered the partially-lit room filled with bunk beds, old carpets, and thick curtains, I whispered, "Where am I?"

A confident woman approached and said in perfect English, "Welcome to Evin Prison, or as many of us like to call it, Evin University."

"University?" I asked with confusion.

The woman chuckled and explained, "Well, you practically have to have a Ph.D. to wind up here. So what's your story?"

"I wish I knew," I replied.

***

My new home was a bleak prison surrounded by menacing walls topped with barbed wire. Any opportunity for escape was next to impossible since watchtowers and armed guards surrounded this nightmare.

There were about twenty-five of us crammed into a twenty-square-meter cell. Sometimes if I was lucky, I could peek out the crack of a window and see a dreary mountain range that covered a large area in the north.

The authorities didn't know what to do with me. Thus, I avoided the initial hazing process that most endure: a softening phase which included solitary confinement. Prisoners were frequently dragged from cells for interrogation where torture was typically applied.

In many ways, waiting your turn and knowing that your fellow detainees are suffering verbal abuse, and infinite other horrors is equally terrorizing. It's like subsisting in a slaughterhouse.

My routine at Evin was fairly structured, but consisted of daily prayers and reading the Quran, which I rather enjoyed. I had grown accustomed to the monotony and lost track of time, which was easy since there were no clocks. I relied on what scarce light poured through the windows to indicate the time. Or, I paid attention to our schedule.

We were always hungry since there was never enough food. Thus, waiting for meal time, like hungry strays, was our only motivation and reward for living in such dire conditions. In the dining hall there were television sets where I watched religious sermons while nibbling small portions of dishes consisting of soya, lentils, and rice.

It was difficult for me to see because my vision was poor. It was apparent that I needed eyeglasses, but that was a luxury I couldn't afford. It was an inconvenience that didn't concern my captors. Thankfully, my other senses had become more acute. My hearing was so sharp that I often wanted to scream, "shut-up," as the noise was so chaotic. And I always felt nauseous and wanted to vomit from the odor that permeated the prison.

Mostly we felt weak from malnutrition. The other women complained about the scarcity of meat. Sometimes, they would fight over measly morsels of chicken bones. I didn't desire flesh and was happy with my vegetarian rations, which I would attempt to stomach while watching rodents scurry into corners. I sometimes wondered if these creatures ever ended up in our meals.

My more fortunate cellmates received money from their families outside the walls which allowed them to purchase extra rations and other benefits. The only things I had to trade were the scraps of meat on my tray and what little I knew about the outside world: the Chinese hospital, the dusty road trip, the restaurant, and hotel. None of this information impressed my cellmates.

CHAPTER 11

It was now winter. According to my cellmates, summers were awful. After all, there was only one shower available for up to two-hundred prisoners. Thus, in hot months, odors were far more pungent, and cockroaches ran rampantly.

I didn't look forward to the future. It was little comfort knowing that this was as good as it gets.

There was very little space, so the other women and I had to share beds. Huddled together like farm animals, we exchanged stories. We talked about ancient Persian history, our families, and life outside of Evin.

As much as the women wanted to vent against the current political regime, they dared not. They refrained from discussing their grandparents' stories about life under Mossadegh when Tehran was a flourishing modern city. Or the following challenges when the Shah took over. At least, if they did, it was only in faint whispers.

One day I heard Darya say, "Don't you think totalitarian regimes throughout the world are more similar to one another than the cultures they take root in?"

Gina nodded and said, "Absolutely, the current Islamic

State doesn't represent true Iranian culture."

"What do you mean?" I asked innocently.

Gina continued, "Current dictatorships must be contextualized against the backdrop of post-colonial politics."

"I don't understand," I responded.

"It's easy to blame the Ayatollah and now Rouhani for our problems, but they're just men," Gina continued.

"But these men are treating us horribly," I protested. "Look at where we are."

"The issues are systemic. They can and do happen anywhere," Darya explained.

"Miss, how are you?" Gina asked. Everyone called me Miss since I thought it was my name. After all, it's what Fan and Jia, the Chinese nurses, had called me.

"I'm good," I answered with a smile.

"Are you starting to remember anything?" Darya asked.

I shook my head.

"What about anything from your childhood," Gina suggested.

"Not really," I whispered, but in fact my mind was starting to feel sharper despite the conditions of the prison, lack of hygiene, and poor nutrition. Perhaps it was because I was no longer highly medicated or maybe my survival instincts were finally kicking in. After all, I was no longer a coddled patient in a remote hospital. I barely remembered anything, but my dreams revealed fragments of the past.

Suddenly, waves of nausea overwhelmed me. Maybe it was the heat or the stress of trying to remember the past, but I felt dizzy and light headed.

A female guard escorted me to the bathroom down a dark, narrow hall. The bathroom floors were cold tiles and I shivered as I crept into a stall and began heaving.

CHAPTER 12
2017

The Hong Kong International Airport was typically efficient as Aaron and Daniel headed toward security. Aaron handed the cleaning ladies his unopened bottles of water.

"*Xia Xia*," the women exclaimed.

"Can't believe you brought that," Daniel grumbled.

"I like to stay hydrated," Aaron retorted.

"Then why didn't you drink it beforehand?"

"Petersen, are you my Mom?"

At that moment, the security machines bleeped, and guards pulled Daniel over.

"Sir, what's in your bag?"

Daniel rifled through his stuff and found a sharp pair of scissors which the guards confiscated.

"Ha, you're one to talk," joked Aaron.

The men grabbed their carry-on and headed toward the escalators of the pristine airport. They whipped past the modern glass architecture and stunning advertisements of Western models selling luxury products.

"We'd better run," Aaron ordered.

"Hey, it's not my fault we're late," Daniel snapped.

Panting, the two ran through the large, crowded airport.

"Man, I'm out of shape," Daniel admitted when they reached their gate. He breathed deeply and felt a burning sensation in his chest.

"Yeah, you should work out more," Aaron suggested while laughing.

The two entered a very long line, while a heaving Daniel implored, "Can you finish your story?"

Ignoring the request, Aaron asked, "Hey did you pack the right clothes for this trip?"

"So who's the mom now?

"I've got some clothes you can have."

"What? Why do you keep giving me stuff?" Daniel demanded.

"No reason," Aaron replied.

"So let's finish the story?"

"Where were we?"

"You were at the club."

Aaron nodded. "Yeah, so …"

Flashback — Shanghai, 2009

I followed Lana out the club. The rain had stopped but the streets were still wet. She sauntered through the cobblestone alleyway like a cat, agile in her heels.

While walking through the streets, I pointed out some of the women in the area and said, "Whenever I'm here those types always approach me."

Lana nodded. "They're stunning. They look like models."

I didn't respond as we entered an empty club on the top of a plaza. Lana marched to the center of the floor and started dancing. I was tense because people were staring.

But unexpectedly when I had my eyes turned away, I felt Lana move closer. She placed her hands on my chest, stood on her tiptoes and kissed my lips.

Aaron and Daniel were now seated on the plane.

Daniel practically spilled his water as he snapped, "Yuck. Why'd she do that?"

Aaron shrugged and looked up to observe the attractive flight crew as they gave safety instructions. He ogled one particularly attractive attendant who looked young enough to be his daughter. Finally, he sighed and said, "The woman couldn't keep her hands off me."

Daniel wailed, "I can't believe she kissed you within the first hour."

Aaron nodded. "Yeah, me neither."

"The most I ever got from Lana was a backhanded compliment."

"I meant, I thought she'd have kissed me sooner."

"Like most women?" Daniel asked sarcastically.

"Yep."

"Whatever," Daniel muttered. "Can we get back to the story?"

Flashback — Shanghai, 2009

At the club, Lana's friends arrived. She introduced us, but then left for the washroom. I was happy to flirt with her friends since they were very cute.

Eventually Lana returned and whispered nervously, "Gosh Aaron, it's getting so crowded, isn't it?"

I chuckled. "If there's ever anarchy, I can protect you."

Lana paused and asked, "Like if I was caught in a riot in Islamabad?"

I was startled. "Why would you be in Pakistan?"

Daniel intently listened to Aaron, but interrupted, "Lana's story is different."

"Oh, yeah?" Aaron asked with a raised eyebrow. He refused to make eye contact with Daniel while ordering a Bloody Mary. He was too focused on the flight attendant's curvy figure.

Daniel rifled through his backpack and pulled out Lana's diary, which he flipped through with ease. "Yep, according to her, you suggested she'd be in Iraq."

Aaron shook his head firmly. "Does that even make sense?"

"Not really," Daniel replied as his face softened.

Aaron continued his story, "We followed Lana's friends to the top floor where she sat on the arm of a sofa."

Flashback — Shanghai, 2009

"Aaron, what was it like growing up in Michigan?"

I shrugged. "Alright."

"Are you from a small town?"

"Yep. How did you know?"

She smiled. "I can tell."

"And you grew up in big cities?"

"Yes, we moved around a lot."

I nodded. "I did, too."

Lana's eyes flickered with amusement. "Did you have a lot of pen-pals?"

"No."

"Not even one?" she teased.

"I'm not really a pen-pal kind of guy."

Lana tilted her head to the side and asked flirtatiously, "So what kind of a guy are you?" She then offered her drink to me.

As I took a sip, a stranger approached and barked, "Hey man, are you going to buy your own drink?"

Lana jumped to her feet and snapped, "How is this any of your business?" She then stormed off.

I figured she went to the washroom, so I talked to the guy who was surprised by Lana's outburst. He turned out to be friends with Lana's group and was a decent guy.

After about fifteen minutes, I realized she wasn't returning. So I ran downstairs and saw Lana laughing with a young waiter who gave her free drinks. I instantly thought — who the hell is this?

They chatted like old friends at the bar next to the dance floor.

When the server saw me approach, his eyes widened, and he quickly took off.

I helped myself to Lana's drink while she whispered, "I hope I didn't say something to upset Jack."

It was evident that this Jack guy left because of me. So I snickered and said, "Don't worry about it."

"Why?" she asked, suddenly nervous.

I pulled her onto the center of the dance floor and replied, "Because you're with me." I danced around Lana but crouched lower to make her feel less threatened.

Lana rapidly blinked as she analyzed me with curiosity. "You have the same color eyes as I do."

I laughed. "Yeah, I was noticing that earlier."

"They're the color of mud, right?"

"Sure."

Lana said excitedly, "Someone once told me that hazel is a sign of impurity."

"Who?"

"Some guy."

"Figures," I said and continued dancing with her.

She blushed. "I need to go to the Ladies' room."

"Sure."

"I'll be right back," she promised and took off.

I waited on the empty dance floor. Minutes passed until a pretty local approached.

"What's your name?" I asked the petite girl. Her bleached blonde hair emphasized her dark complexion. "Mei Li," she responded with a big smile.

"That means beautiful, right?"

She nodded.

"It suits you," I teased.

Me Li giggled flirtatiously and inched closer to me.

I started to put my arm around her waist when I looked up and saw Lana. She shot me a cold look and dashed out of the club.

I laughed, but then chased her out the door into the middle of the street and joked, "You look jealous."

"Hardly," she snapped. Even though it was the middle of the night, the city was sweltering. As Lana anxiously glanced toward the street, I could see beads of sweat forming on her white neck. She must have noticed because she pulled up her hair and said, "I need a hair band."

"I have one back at my hotel," I replied.

"Very funny," Lana said and ran to a row of taxis.

I ran after her, "Give me your number. I'll call you."

Lana quickly handed me her card before slipping into the taxi.

This woman was complicated. One minute she was flirting, kissing me, and sharing her drink. The next, she was upset. Evidently Lana was jealous of the little blonde.

How typical, I thought. She wasn't as sophisticated as she pretended to be.

Daniel was laughing so hard that he accidentally hit the arm of another passenger, scattering peanuts across the aisle. The guy gave Aaron and Daniel an irritated glance.

"It's not that funny," Aaron growled. "Quit throwing stuff."

Daniel calmed down and said, "Hey, man, we've all been there."

Aaron nodded.

"Thing is; Lana didn't seem jealous when Curt flirted with his secretary."

Aaron shrugged. "Guess she didn't like Curt much."

Daniel looked doubtful.

"Anyway, whose version are you going to believe?"

Daniel pulled out the diary and said, "According to Lana, you followed her to a clothing market in 2015."

Aaron shook his head. "Nope, she first approached me. I didn't expect ever to see Lana again and went on with my life. But in 2015, I was back in Shanghai."

Flashback — Shanghai, 2015

I was speaking at a biotech conference about biomedical devices.

After finishing my presentation, a round of questions began.

I heard a woman's voice ask, "Mr. Walker, what did you mean by your assertion that China is a great place for science?"

I looked at the woman. She was wearing a navy-blue suit and had her hair pulled up.

Attendees stared at her.

I answered, "We can conduct experiments here that we can't in the U.S. or Europe."

"Can you clarify that?"

"Um, sure," I replied with hesitation.

"Vivisections?"

Folks in the audience chuckled. People who'd been asleep were suddenly wide-awake realizing there was controversy.

I shook my head and said, "Stem cell research requires the use of —"

She interjected, "Human life."

"Honey, you gotta have an open mind."

The audience was aroused. One guy yelled, "Lady, lighten up." Others mumbled, "I hate women like her."

She turned red, clenched her jaw, and sat back down. I suddenly realized it was Lana.

After the presentation, I noticed her leaving so I followed and said, "Hey, I didn't mean to upset you."

"I'm not upset," she protested.

Lana's features were now more chiseled. She looked very sophisticated. I sensed her overwhelming confidence, so I decided to cut her down to make myself feel more powerful. I did this by pretending not to remember her and asked, "You look familiar, have we met?

Lana's eyes widened, and her lips parted. "We hung out in 2009."

I paused for a minute and pretended to rack my memory. Then I exclaimed, "Oh, yeah, you were chubbier."

She bit her lip and looked away.

I grinned. "Hey, sorry I never called you."

Lana shrugged. "I didn't notice. I left a few days later."

I nodded. "Hey, it's been great talking to you, but I've gotta go.

I'm playing soccer with friends."

"Sure, bye," she said walking away.

Daniel listened intently. "So she was after you?"

"They always are," Aaron replied.

"What about the incident when you almost got into a bar fight over Lana?"

"Nah, that's not how it went down —*"*

Flashback — Shanghai, 2015

My soccer buddies and I entered a Moldavian bar hidden in a dark alleyway. It was a secret spot. So I was surprised to see Lana in the corner with a group of Eastern Europeans. They were angry and yelling words like "Maidan" and "Donbass." I expected Lana to argue back, but she was surprisingly calm. She responded with a measured tone, but upon seeing us, the Slavs left in a hurry, which seemed suspicious.

An hour later, we headed over to a Chinese club that wasn't popular with foreigners. I was surprised to see Lana again. This time she was by the bar talking with a man and a woman who left as my friends and I sat down at a corner table.

Lana remained alone at the bar. She was reading texts, so I approached and joked, "You look lonely."

She glanced up and replied, "I wish."

I motioned for the waiter and ordered a couple shots of tequila.

"Hey, who were your friends?" I asked.

Lana refused the shot, but replied, "Mina is a flight attendant for Emirates and her boyfriend David works for Bechtel."

"Cool."

"Mina's father is Egyptian, and David's dad is Iraqi."

"You don't want a drink?"

"I really can't," Lana protested.

"Why not?"

"Not in the mood," she replied, rudely pushing past me and jumping on the stage to dance.

Chinese hip-hop remixes were blasting. Lana wasn't very friendly, so I went back to my friends. A group of attractive women sat at our table, so I focused on them. When I glanced at the stage, I saw Lana watching. Her eyes narrowed. I laughed because she obviously didn't like being ignored. So, I continued pretending she wasn't there.

I flirted with a waitress until I saw Lana heading for the exit. I waited a few seconds, and then chased her out the door to the row of taxis waiting outside the club.

Lana turned to me as if she'd expected I'd follow. She paused, glanced around the busy street, and said, "I'd rather walk home."

I nodded.

"Come with me, Aaron. I want to talk."

"Talk?" I asked with a grin.

"Yes," she replied.

We walked through the alleys without saying much. I listened to the clicking of her heels. Finally, she joked, "I thought we'd braid each other's hair and share quilt making tips."

I groaned. "I don't think we're on the same wavelength."

"Indeed, we're diametrically opposed."

I smiled.

Lana continued, "You're certainly not the type of guy I normally hang out with."

"Oh, yeah?" I asked sarcastically. I expected her to give me an elitist diatribe about how she's only friends with people who move in her exclusive circles.

Instead, she said, "I barely know you, but I realized when we met that you grew up fighting against adversity and you've gotten so much further than a lot."

"Not really," I confessed thinking about my business troubles.

"You've never had it easy which is why you're so strong."

"I also work out a lot," I joked.

"I also love that we don't run in the same circles."

I didn't say anything.

"Because I don't trust my friends and acquaintances," Lana continued.

"Yet you trust a stranger?"

Lana nodded. "I have no expectations of you."

"Cool."

We were now at her apartment complex. While entering the glass doors and heading to the high-speed elevators, we passed the front desk in the lobby. An uptight concierge eyed me suspiciously.

Lana smiled and joked, "Zhè shì wǒ dí gēgē."

The concierge raised an eyebrow as if to say, "Yeah right, he's not your brother."

"Very funny," I said to Lana in the elevator.

"Thank you. It's never easy being the funniest person in the room."

"Luckily, you'll never have that problem."

Lana playfully punched my upper arm. "It takes a sophisticated person to appreciate my humor."

"Don't you mean special?"

When we reached her floor, I didn't pay much attention to the décor because I was too focused on Lana's methodical movements. Luxurious settings were so standard in Chinese first-tier cities that I took them for granted.

However, I observed that apart from the customized fixtures, the furnishings chosen by Lana were simple, yet elegant. In the corner was a teak shelf covered in books about ancient history. Antiques throughout the room were distinct from the modern designs popular in new money households. The room smelled of chilled orchids. I relaxed because this atmosphere was an improvement from the club.

An awkward silence developed and tension grew as Lana threw her purse on the dining table and said, "Please have a seat."

I sat down on her white sofa. A cat jumped onto my lap.

Lana sauntered past us, removed her linen jacket, and said, "His name is Peter."

"You named your cat Peter?"

Lana closed the balcony windows. She pulled up her hair and whispered, "Gosh, it's hot isn't it?"

I observed sweat dripping from her neck. I didn't say anything as she switched on the air-conditioning. Her white silk blouse was wet and left little to the imagination.

"What do you want to drink?" she asked as she headed into the *kitchen.*

"Coffee," I replied.

"Cream and sugar?"

"Just black."

As Lana returned to the living room with a tray, she asked, "Why were you annoyed when I warned you about taxi drivers in Beijing?

"You remember a lot about that night," I remarked.

"Yes, I remember everything you said."

I grinned and studied her carefully.

She continued, "I always remember what people say."

I shrugged. "I don't remember much about that night."

Lana's lashes batted rapidly as she fought to conceal disappointment.

With a smirk, I said, "I don't remember things if I don't think I'll ever see someone again.

Lana nodded, took a deep breath, and looked away.

Peter purred loudly. He had big green eyes and a flat nose, so I asked, "Hey, what happened to your cat's nose? It's flat."

Lana ignored my question as Peter jumped off my lap. She sat down on the carpet and began to stroke his exposed belly. She looked up at me and said, "I'm sorry I was rude when we met."

"I don't remember," I reminded her.

"I attacked your ancestors."

"Yeah, that wasn't very nice."

"I could explain why, but you probably don't want to know."

"Yeah, I don't."

Lana batted her eyes rapidly. Her hands trembled. It was like she didn't know what to say. Suddenly as if to fill the void, she babbled, "When Cleopatra first met Caesar at fourteen, she didn't know who he was, but she warned him to watch out for the Romans."

I stared because her cheeks flushed as she talked. "At least according to George Bernard Shaw, the famous —"

"Irish play right," I finished her sentence. "Yeah, I know who he is."

Lana smiled while cradling Peter on the floor. She seemed out of character — demure and almost vulnerable while looking up at me.

Peter escaped from her arms and ran back to me.

As he crawled into my lap, Lana gasped, "Gosh, Aaron, Peter generally doesn't like men."

I raised an eyebrow. "You bring a lot of guys back here?"

Lana's face reddened. "Goodness, never. You're the first."

"Sure," I replied sarcastically. "Then who are these men?"

"Just my husband and his business partner Ben."

I suddenly noticed her left hand.

Husband? Jesus — I thought. Why the hell hadn't I noticed the rock and thick wedding band earlier? I was generally very observant. Then again, everything about Lana's style of dress and apartment was unassuming.

I guess I was so caught in the moment and fixated on Lana's overtly seductive qualities.

I jumped up, spilling coffee on Lana's silk sofa. Peter scratched my pants as he fell to the floor.

This woman was drama; the last thing I needed was an angry husband after me. So I snapped, "Hey, I've gotta go."

Lana nodded, picked up her cat, and said, "Sure, I understand."

Then I got the hell out of there.

Daniel nodded while listening and said, "Interesting."

"Yeah," Aaron agreed.

"I was at the bar and grill when you showed up and picked a fight with that Brazilian journalist, Tomas."

Aaron was evasive. "Sure, I saw Lana on other occasions. Why were you there?

"I was spying on Lana for Ben and Steiger. I was with them when they confronted Lana."

"Steiger confronted Lana publicly?"

"Yeah," Daniel replied. "Steiger's driver took pictures of you two together. He was furious thinking you'd had an affair."

"What exactly did she say?"

"Lana said you promised to take her to find her parents

in Beijing."

Aaron took a deep breath and began, "After the coffee ordeal at Lana's place, I went home."

Flashback — Guangzhou, 2015

I had been successful, but by 2011, business was down. In 2008, when the recession hit the U.S., we didn't suffer immediately. But within a few years, it was hard to sustain a profit. I could barely get out of the red. So I took over a security company with some other guys from my Iraq days. I let my father handle the investigations and client relations.

When I got back, Dad told me about a new assignment involving a girl named Natalia Canaan. Apparently, her parents had disappeared in Kuala Lumpur back in the 90s when she was still a kid. Dad had a major grudge because he was certain that Natalia's father had traded secrets with the Viet Cong in order to secure his own release which resulted in the deaths of many American soldiers.

Some private company hired us to escort Natalia Canaan to a site in the middle of China, not far from Beijing. It was just for questioning, so I didn't think much about the assignment and headed to the gym.

After my workout, I returned to our warehouse and grabbed a seat at Dad's desk. I browsed through the file and read the report. But when I saw the picture of Natalia, I dropped the stack of papers.

There was no mistake about it, Natalia Canaan was Lana Hayaak. Tension gripped my chest as thoughts raced through my head. Was it an accident that I met Lana? Was she stalking me? Did she know that I was supposed to be hunting her?

Lana seemed nothing like the woman described in the report. Natalia Canaan was someone I could almost relate to. Both our dads had been in Vietnam. Her parents were DEA. Then Natalia lived in near poverty as a teenager. She'd struggled in her early twenties while I'd spent my youth in Iraq watching my buddies get blown to bits.

How did a nice girl turn into such a royal pain in my ass? I thought I was done with Hayaak, but now she was my target. I'd have loved to turn down this assignment. But we needed the money and this paid well.

So I returned to Shanghai. I quickly figured out that Lana was scheduled to attend an event at the Four Seasons. Some Governor from the U.S. was in town.

I hung out in the lobby talking to the Governor's security guys and then saw Lana exit the ballroom. I followed her to the market where I watched her shop for cheongsam dresses. When she walked out of a stall, I said, "Hey what was the other night about?"

Lana glanced away and paid the clerk.

"I didn't know you were married," I shouted.

She shrugged. "I always wear my ring."

"So why was I at your place?"

Lana finally turned to me. "I wanted to talk."

"Yeah, right!"

"There are things I need to tell you."

"I don't want to know."

"Then why are you here?"

"Why do you hang out in bars with strangers" I demanded.

"You're so funny," she taunted.

"Seriously, I'm curious."

"I'm a people person," she joked dryly.

"You're a married woman," I reminded her.

"And you're a married man, so I guess we've got a lot in common."

"How did you know I'm married?"

"The Internet."

"Hey, I don't have to explain myself," I shouted.

Chinese shopkeepers gathered nearby. We'd created quite scene. A small crowd stared and whispered.

I continued, "What am I — a pawn in one of your games?"

Lana didn't say anything but looked down with shame as I talked. "I won't get mixed up in a love triangle."

Then a middle-aged couple approached.

The woman exclaimed, "Lana, how nice to see you!"

"Oh, hi, Vivian," Lana responded nervously.

"Who's your friend?" Vivian eyed me up and down.

"Um, Aaron is my brother."

"Really, he doesn't seem like a brother," Vivian remarked while studying me.

"I mean, a cousin," Lana clarified.

"I see," said the older woman skeptically.

Lana fought to regain her composure. However, her hair was a mess, and her cheeks flushed.

She finally said, "Aaron, this is Vivian and her husband, Tim."

I smiled broadly. "How do you like Shanghai?"

***

After Lana's friends left, she turned to me and whispered, "Walker, I have to ask you something." She picked up her bags, and we walked out of the store toward the escalator.

"Just ask," I replied. It was like Lana had figured out that I was on to her past.

"Do you throw balls around because you enjoy it or because society expects it?"

"What?" I exclaimed.

"Sports, why do you play?"

Her questions didn't make sense. Was she deflecting to avoid discussing her husband?

Finally, I responded, "I like it."

"I've never understood games involving inanimate objects."

I exhaled. "There's a feeling of power when you have a ball firmly gripped in your hands."

"As a girl, I deplored playing sports."

"Glad to know you were born a girl; otherwise I wouldn't be sure."

Lana ignored my joke and said dreamily, "I wished I'd been born in a different era, one where girls weren't expected to be like men."

"You had it rough," I replied sarcastically.

Lana nodded. We walked past rows of stalls selling scarves, handbags, and electronics.

Dealers jumped out and chanted, "Would you like to buy a

watch?"

We ignored them as they displayed images of extravagant counterfeits.

Lana continued, "You were always picked first for any team."

"Weren't you?"

She was quiet for a second, but then confessed, "Yes, but for completely different reasons."

"Does it matter?"

"When we met, you felt so familiar."

"Oh, yeah."

"And, yet so different," Lana paused for a moment, glanced into my eyes, and gasped. "I'd never seen anyone like you."

I chuckled. I should have held my gaze, but instead, blurted, "You hadn't?"

She immediately turned away, but said, "I felt a certain connection."

"Come on Lana. You're too sophisticated for that."

She stopped in the center of the dirty ground floor and stared at me.

"Walker, I didn't mean that kind of 'connection.' We have no chemistry," she declared with a slight grin.

I raised an eyebrow. "Who are you trying to convince — yourself or me?"

My eyes dropped for a second.

Lana immediately snapped her fingers in my face. "Walker, eyes up here."

"Huh?" I murmured, returning to her eyes which narrowed.

"You're not my type," she declared.

I rolled my eyes.

"I feel like we share history," she continued.

I froze wondering if Lana knew about my assignment. It would explain this erratic conversation. Then again, she was always somewhat quirky.

But then she said, "After all, you served in Iraq and I have a Bachelors in Middle Eastern studies."

"Not exactly the same thing," I remarked, not sure where she was

going with this.

Maybe Lana didn't know that I knew her real name was Natalia Canaan and that our fathers had been arch enemies during their tours in Vietnam.

"You know so much more about the world," she said as her face softened.

"Do you mean Iraq?"

"Yes, but also your work in China."

"Okay."

"There's only so much anyone can ever learn from a book or in an office."

"Yep," I agreed.

"So you know more than I ever will," Lana said, batting her eyes and tilting her head slightly to the side.

She had a point. I'd seen a hell of a lot more than the bureaucrats in Washington or any of the suits at any corporate headquarters. Lawyers could read and write about conflicts in the manufacturing sector, but how many had stepped foot in a factory? Plus, I'd been around the world, but not the places featured in tourist brochures.

"You seem smart." We exited through glass doors and stood on the busy street corner.

It was hard to talk with motorcycles whizzing by or cars blasting their horns, but Lana tried "I'm smart enough to know my limitations."

"That's more than most."

"Walker, what do you read?"

"The news and stuff."

"What about the Bible?"

"Not really into that."

"I read the Bible when I was five," Lana shared.

"So you're a believer?" I asked with a grin.

She took a step backward and said, "It was the only book I wasn't supposed to read."

"Why? Were your parents Commies?"

Lana's face tensed, she refused to make eye contact and looked toward the curb. Her driver had pulled up, and she whispered, "I

better go."
    "*Sure, bye," I said.*
    "*Take care, Aaron, I'll talk to you later."*

"You talked to Lana. A lot," Daniel noted.

"Sure, but not the way Lana described it in her diary."

"Alright," Daniel conceded, "we've established that the woman is a liar."

"Truth stretcher," Aaron clarified.

"What about the train to Beijing?"

"What about it?"

"It was the last time anyone saw her."

"Uh, huh," Aaron said looking at his watch. The flight had been in transit for more than four hours. "Look, Daniel, I need to take a nap." Aaron pulled out a pillow and turned to his side.

"Um, sure."

"We'll finish this later, alright?"

"No problem." Daniel turned to the entertainment section and flipped through in-flight movies. He settled for *Wonder Woman.*

CHAPTER 13

Tehran, Iran — 2016

Lana Hayaak

I felt sedated: as if I'd been asleep for a century. As I forced my eyes open, I surmised I was lying in a single bed without any companions. I glanced around and was relieved to discover that I was no longer in prison. I certainly didn't miss the smell of sulfur, desperation, and fear.

I realized I was now in a very crowded room filled with individuals who were badly wounded. Groggy, I analyzed my new location and acknowledged that I was in a hospital again. However, this one wasn't as empty or sterile as the one in China.

A doctor with round eyes, olive skin, and a gray beard approached cautiously. He looked genuinely concerned as he gently clasped my hands and introduced himself.

"My dear, my name is Dr. Hamid."

I batted my eyes and chirped, "It's so lovely to meet you."

"It's nice to meet you."

"Doctor," I chatted gaily, "I finally remember something."

"What do you remember?" he inquired earnestly.

"The cat's name is Dinah."

Dr. Hamid stared at me as I exclaimed, "I dreamt of cats and talking mice who cried. *Would you like cats, if you were me?* To which I said, *I wish I could show you our cat, Dinah. I think you'd take a fancy to cats if you could see her. She is such a dear thing.*"

Dr. Hamid nodded and said, "That's very good my dear."

I smiled and asked, "Is everything alright doctor?"

The doctor's face became serious as he replied, "My dear, I have some grave news to share."

I started laughing hysterically. Dr. Hamid looked alarmed, and fellow patients glanced over with confusion.

"Don't tell me … I'm pregnant?"

He nodded. "Yes, you are with child. But Miss …"

"What?" I demanded.

Dr. Hamid hesitated, took a deep breath and whispered, "You have a brain tumor."

"So, I'm dying?"

Dr. Hamid nodded.

"Why are you laughing?" he asked with concern.

"At least I'll be free," I replied. After all, the world I'd known these past several months was hell. My only escape was in my dreams, but it was nearly impossible to sleep in a room filled with other bodies tossing and turning from anxiety.

Doctor Hamid nodded and said, "I understand."

I turned away and stared out the window at the arid land. I noticed a sparrow land on the window sill. Even Persian birds have a certain charm, I thought.

I then began to sing a song to myself that felt like something from my childhood."

I've come all the way from Carthage. I've come a long, long way from home. But I won't go back. Oh, no, I won't go back, until I've battled in the gates of Rome.

I realized that the doctor, some nurses, and other patients were gaping. So I closed my eyes, stopped singing, and dreamt I was running through a meadow with a long-haired cat who had big green eyes, a brick-pink nose, and black paws.

CHAPTER 14

"Hey, watch it," Aaron complained as he was woken by Daniel's elbowing.

Daniel ripped off his headphones and snapped, "Why did you file attempted murder charges against Lana?"

Aaron was groggy, but finally replied, "I was in a lot of trouble."

"Why?"

"The contractor who hired me was furious when I botched the project."

"I bet."

"I lost my whole business," Aaron continued.

"Oh, wow."

"It's for the best. I'm done with all that."

"So what are you doing now?"

"Prepping Trinity to raise funds from Steiger, remember?"

"Yeah, sure," Daniel replied.

"Anyway, let me finish the story. It was foggy when I got to the *Hong Qiao* train station."

Flashback — Train, 2015

I was late because of an argument with Dad. Plus, as I was making my way through the station, I saw a man struggling at the ticket kiosk. He was elderly and both his hands were missing. I've seen my share of men without limbs, but I never get used to it. So I took the time to put some RMB in the bucket he cradled in between his shoulders and finished his transaction. The man nodded graciously and said Xia Xia repeatedly as I realized boarding was almost finished.

Lana was already on the train when I arrived. She looked anxious.

I sat down across from her and teased, "You're more uptight than usual."

She stared out the window and didn't say anything, so I waved the waiter over and ordered a bottle of vodka.

"Isn't it rather early to drink?"

"Lana, it's already 5 p.m. Relax."

The woman needed alcohol badly.

I joked. "Did you sleep 'til noon?"

She was tense and snapped, "I'm being set up."

"You sound paranoid."

"Yesterday before I got to Curt's party, I met with a supervisor. He claims that over a million dollars was wired to my bank account."

My eyes widened. "Well, lucky you."

Lana shook her head. "I can't touch that money. Even if I wanted to…"

"China has strict laws against foreign withdrawals. At most you could remove $500 a day."

She nodded and said, "This is a trap."

"Set by whom?"

"Not sure. Maybe you know?"

"I wish, but I've told you all I know."

Lana nodded. "Your dad hates my parents. He thinks they got what they deserved."

"C'mon, why do you care what anyone thinks?"

"Because I'm a target! I was set up, and now I get to take the fall."

"What were you involved in?"

Lana took a sip of water and answered carefully, "It's complex."

I studied her carefully. "Why is everything so complicated with you?"

"My upbringing was complicated," she replied sarcastically.

"Apparently."

"We can't all be as lucky as you, Walker."

"Lucky? What are you talking about?"

"Never mind."

"Lana, I was the only Asian kid within thousands of miles."

"So?"

"You went to international schools."

"Indeed. For the first fifteen years of my life, I was constantly told I was special."

"This is why you're upset?"

"Yes, my childhood was a joke."

"People dream of your problems."

"You're missing my point."

"You have one?"

"There was nothing special about my schoolmates or me. We were just reaping the benefits of imperialism."

I leaned forward. "So what have you done?"

"Sovereign nations have a right to self-defense."

"What have you done," I repeated, staring firmly at her.

Nervously, she blurted, "Shared technology trade secrets."

"Why?"

"I've always had a soft spot for the other side."

I groaned. "So you're guilty of treason?"

"Under laws created by a Byzantine system that contradict what it purports to achieve."

"Look I'm not judging. I'm concerned about you."

"You are?" Lana asked with surprise.

"Yeah, let's run away together," I joked.

"Seriously?" she asked with a raised eyebrow.

"Sure, we could go to Brazil."

Lana looked wistful as she paused and whispered, "There're no extradition laws for Americans in Brazil." She almost smiled, but then suddenly her eyes narrowed. "Does that line ever work?"

"Huh?"

"Don't insult my intelligence."

I stared at the woman.

"Walker, the only trip we'll ever take together is the one to hell."

"Seriously, Lana? If anyone uses lines and flirty comments, it's you."

Her face softened.

I exhaled. "So what'll you do?"

"Join my old boss, Peter."

"Yeah, but he probably set you up."

"I don't think so," she said without conviction.

Lana looked away and out the window, but it was impossible to see anything.

"Come with me," I suggested.

"So you can hand me off?"

"That won't happen," I promised.

"You don't have a choice."

"If you knew this, why'd you come?"

"I wanted to say goodbye."

"Why?"

Lana shrugged. "I think you're an okay guy."

"What you're doing is wrong," I told her.

Lana looked me in the eye and declared, "I'll die for my principles."

"Probably," I agreed.

"It's better to die for something than to live for nothing."

I didn't say anything because I had no idea what I wanted anymore. I'd spent half my life following orders. Lana was tenacious about something I'd never understand.

So instead I joked, "Lana, just admit you're in love with me."

"What?"

"You've been obsessed with me ever since we met."

She gasped and said dryly, "Yeah, I've cried myself to sleep over you for the past six years."

"You wouldn't be the first."

"You're unbelievable!" she snapped while jumping up.

"Hey, where are you going?"

Lana grabbed her stuff, turned to me, and said "You're not my type."

I rolled my eyes. "And Steiger is?"

"My marriage is none of your business," she replied, taking a step towards me.

"You both belong together."

"Why?" she asked with surprise.

"You're both so power-hungry," I replied.

I was expecting her to slap me, but suddenly she leaned in and kissed me.

Her mouth tasted bitter like poison, and I quickly felt numb everywhere. The train became blurry. I was disoriented and stumbled forward, trying to follow Lana.

I was groggy, but could hear the train intercom system announce a stop. As I fell over, I glanced up and saw Lana running for the door. I kept thinking she'd look back at me, but she didn't. She just kept running.

Instinctively, I knew we'd never see one another again. She knew it, too. So why didn't she look back?

Daniel nodded. "Cause, she wasn't that into you."

"Fuck you, Petersen."

"Hey, I thought you didn't care."

"I don't."

"Oh, yeah, you filed attempted murder charges against her. That was harsh."

Aaron shook his head. "I only did it to keep Steiger and the client off my back. The poison hardly affected me."

Daniel nodded. "Okay."

"When I woke, the train was almost in Beijing. I

stumbled around and found Lana's purse under my foot."

"Hmm," Daniel murmured. "That's odd."

"Yeah, I was surprised she left it."

"Did you go after her?"

"Yeah, but I'd been asleep for hours. It took half a day to get back to where Lana had jumped. Then I spent all night tracking her."

"Did you find anything?"

Aaron nodded. "Lana's cat."

"Peter?"

"Yeah, he was dirty and near death."

"Where is he?"

"Trinity has him." Aaron whipped out his phone and revealed pictures of his sister holding a gray cat with green eyes and a flat brick-colored nose. It certainly looked like Peter.

Daniel shook his head and said, "Crazy, but man that's a fat cat."

Aaron laughed, "Yeah, Peter gained a lot of weight after Trinity adopted him."

"Apparently," Daniel noted with slight disgust.

"It wasn't easy smuggling him out of China," Aaron confessed.

Daniel looked annoyed as he exclaimed, "You should've turned Peter over to the authorities. He was evidence."

"Yeah, evidence of her death," Aaron snapped.

Daniel paused for a moment. "Lana would never have left her cat."

"Exactly, but as long as there was a chance Lana was still alive, an investigation would continue."

"True," Daniel agreed.

"Besides, no one gave a damn about Peter. My sister loves cats."

"What was in her purse?"

"Flash drives."

"What was on them?"

Aaron accepted water from the flight attendant, drank quickly, and replied, "Codes that I couldn't decipher. I handed them over to the U.S. Embassy."

"That's what Lana wanted you to do."

"Yeah, maybe," Aaron agreed.

"Do you think it was an accident Lana met you?"

"I saw her before she ever saw me."

"Maybe, but maybe Lana saw an opportunity in you."

"You think she used me?"

"Yeah," Daniel asserted.

"I don't think so."

"Why?"

"She was so intense. You can't fake those feelings."

Daniel rolled his eyes, put on his headphones, and began watching *Spider-Man*.

Aaron turned to Daniel and snapped angrily, "Lana is dead and you're whining about her intent?"

"It matters."

"This is all about you again."

"Huh."

"You just want to believe that Lana secretly liked you."

Daniel ignored Aaron and suggested, "Maybe she escaped."

"Not likely," Aaron responded tersely.

"How can you be so certain?"

"My gut."

"So Lana meant nothing to you?"

"Absolutely nothing," Aaron replied. He then pulled out a pillow and fell asleep against the window. While sleeping, he dreamt about conversations he hadn't bothered to share with Daniel.

Later, he woke and reviewed a torn passage from Lana's diary which had been sewn into her purse:

"Reason compelled me to leave immediately, but as I fought to escape his gaze.

I couldn't help looking into his eyes, because they reminded me so much of my own.

For years, he reminded me of someone I once cared about, me."

CHAPTER 15
Tehran, Iran — 2016
Lana

Lying in the hospital bed, I could feel my swollen belly. It was huge since I would give birth any day. I stared at my tray of food which contained lentil soup, cherry juice, dried apples, and rice. But I couldn't eat these days. If I did, I became nauseous and vomited all over myself and anyone who approached.

My vision was almost completely gone, so I could barely see, let alone read anymore. If I were lucky, the nurses would read the Quran to me. I tried to make out the images in my room, but it was a blur. I generally focused on listening to the sounds that seemed louder than ever: birds chirping, the humming of the fan, chatter by other patients, or the loud noises of objects dropped in the hospital. And my acute sense of smell only aggravated by nausea.

I felt hot and sticky from the sweat that covered my gown and the bed sheets.

Doctor Hamid sat nearby and asked, "Are you in a lot of pain?"

"Yes."

"I'll get you some more pain reliever."

"Thank you, Doctor."

"Miss, I have to ask you a personal question."

I didn't say anything because I didn't like questions. They reminded me of interrogations.

Slowly, Doctor Hamid asked, "Do you know who the father of your child is?"

I felt so stressed by this question that my body immediately tensed.

Doctor Hamid cautioned me not to exert unnecessary energy. "Take it easy."

I shook my head slowly. Tears welled in my eyes, and I cried, "I still can't remember anything."

"It's okay."

"What will happen to my baby?"

"Don't worry. We'll take care of it."

"But what if it's a girl?" I asked.

"Iran has more educated women than any country in the region, perhaps even the world."

"So she'll grow up to be a doctor like you?"

"Sure, but how do you know it's a girl?"

"Just a feeling," I replied as I drifted to sleep.

I dreamt that I was in a cottage in the middle of a meadow in the country. Inside a Tudor style home, I sat at an oak dining table by the fire. I was nervous and excited, but said to an older woman, "Ellen, it would be heaven to escape this comfortless and disorderly place."

PART 4
2040

·

CHAPTER 1
Silicon Valley — Palo Alto

Ben Chang brushed gray hair away from his prominent cheekbones. He sat at his oak desk in a brightly lit office sorting through documents when a tall blonde barged through the door.

Curt Steiger was now in his sixties, but retained his youthful intensity. He rushed in and anxiously exclaimed, "Ben you'll never believe it."

"Believe what?" Ben asked with a raised eyebrow.

"I saw Lana."

"Where?"

"At the pharma conference in South San Francisco."

Ben stared at his partner. "Curt, I'm concerned about you."

"Why?"

"You haven't suffered these Lana delusions in almost a decade."

"I swear it was Lana, except she was wearing a hijab."

Ben sighed and acted as if he was talking to an infant. Changing the subject, he asked, "My friend, aren't you happy being the father of such a fine young man?"

Curt snorted. "That kid is a complete disappointment."

"C'mon, your expectations are too high."

"I accomplished so much more at his age."

"Alexander is a chemistry student at Stanford."

"He's only at Stanford because of me."

"Not everyone has your genius, Curt."

"Sometimes, I wonder if the kid is even mine."

"How can you say such a thing?"

"Easily," snapped Curt. "He was born years before I married Cindy."

"Because you had to wait seven years for Lana to be declared legally dead," Ben reminded his friend.

"Alexander is nothing like me."

Ben sighed.

"The guy posts more selfies than a teenage girl," Curt complained.

"Alexander is very good looking. He could be a male model."

"Yeah, every father's dream"

Ben continued, "Girls adore him."

"Alex has no work ethic, which I blame on his mother," Curt grumbled as he marched out of his office. "Cindy coddles him."

"Hey, where are you going?"

"To find Lana."

Ben shook his head with disappointment and returned to his work.

CHAPTER 2
Stanford University

Priya Patel's toffee colored skin glistened under the fluorescent lights as she sat polishing her latest manuscript in a messy office. After years of working for Steiger Pharmaceuticals, she was now head of the chemistry department. Priya was so immersed in work that she barely noticed Nina Farzad knocking on her open door.

Nina was a slender woman in her early twenties. She wore thick glasses that barely hid her dark cat-shaped eyes adorned with thick lashes. Nina's dark hair was tucked under a black scarf highlighting her pale white skin and full lips.

"Dr. Patel," Nina whispered as she deferentially entered the room.

Without glancing up, the Professor said, "Oh, please call me Priya. No need for formalities." But as Priya looked up and saw Nina, she gasped.

"What is it?" Nina asked with alarm. "You look like you've seen a ghost."

Priya exhaled, jumped up, and exclaimed, "My goodness, it's just that you look so much like someone I

111

knew a very long time ago."

"I see," Nina responded with surprise. She was confused and didn't know what to say.

"Where are you from?"

"Tehran."

"Ah, yes, now I remember. You're our new teaching fellow."

"Yes, I'm delighted to be here."

"You'll be filling in for Professor Ryan this week," Priya explained.

Nina nodded.

Priya sighed, "Alas, you know how undergrads can be. Hopefully, Chem 101 won't bore you too much."

"Not at all. I love the enthusiasm of freshman."

"Ha, ha," Priya laughed sarcastically. "Well, they certainly have energy."

CHAPTER 3
Stanford University

At 6'3", the extremely athletic Alexander Steiger stood out in his chemistry class because his honey colored tan suggested that he spent more time outside than in a lab. He sat in the far back corner of the arena-style classroom with his clique of friends.

The fluorescent overhead lights flickered as Nina Farzad entered the room and took her place behind the podium. Nina barely looked up as she arranged her notes and checked the overhead projector to make sure her slides were in order.

"Hey check out the substitute GTF," Robert whispered.

"Ugh, why do they still dress like that?" George complained.

"C'mon have some respect," Robert ordered.

Alexander didn't say anything because he was too busy staring at Nina. Finally, he remarked, "She doesn't look Arab."

Robert slapped Alexander and said, "Nina isn't an Arab. She's Persian, you moron."

"Whatever," George snapped.

"Farzad doesn't even look Persian," Alexander observed.

"She kind of looks like you," Robert teased as he punched Alexander in the shoulder. "But Nina is pretty."

Indeed, both had high cheekbones and hazel, cat-like eyes.

"Figures that Alex likes someone who looks like himself," George remarked.

"So weird," Robert said with a smirk.

"Both of you, shut up," Alex joked. But under his breath, he muttered, "I'll be stopping by her office hours for sure."

CHAPTER 4
Office Hours

Alex confidently strode into Nina Farzad's office. She was immersed in research, but raised her head and asked, "How can I help you?"

"I'm struggling with chemistry," Alexander confessed.

Nina pulled out her records. "Sorry, what was your name again?"

"Alexander Steiger."

Nina carefully studied Alexander's records, took a deep breath and said, "Ah, yes, chemistry isn't your strength."

Alexander grinned. "Yeah, I'm a natural when it comes to sports."

Nina focused on analyzing Alexander's previous exams.

Alexander continued, "I love the outdoors. What about you?"

Nina ignored his question and said sternly, "Mr. Steiger, chemistry is hard work."

"I don't have an aptitude."

"Aptitude will only get you so far. Chemistry is about how much you're willing to put into it."

"They're going to fail me out of here, aren't they?"

"Yes, if you don't pull up your grades."

"Can you tutor me?" Alexander implored. He flashed Nina a boyish grin.

Nina sighed deeply and replied, "I can't because I'm your GTF and the academic rules forbid it."

"Yeah, but you're only our substitute GTF for this week."

Nina looked back at her paperwork but nodded.

"Please, I can pay you double, triple your normal rate."

Nina didn't say anything but felt slighted because she felt that Alex was flaunting his money. Despite her humble background, she was very proud. At the same time, she wanted to send money to her parents in Iran.

Alexander pulled out a massive wad of cash and said, "Please, I insist."

Nina wanted to say, "Steiger, you can't go through life buying your way out of problems," but she refrained because she knew this wasn't true.

Finally, Nina conceded, "Okay, meet me in front of the science library next Thursday afternoon at 4 p.m. sharp."

"You can't come over to my place?" Alexander asked devilishly.

"I'll see you at the library," Nina repeated.

Alex started to leave, but then took a step back and asked, "One more question."

Vexed, Nina looked up again. "Yes?"

"Do you spend much time with men?"

"What is the point of your question?"

"Did you go to school with guys?"

Nina let out a heavy sigh of exasperation and replied, "No, in Iran women and men learn separately."

"Just what I thought," Alex said with a chuckle as he finally left Nina's office.

CHAPTER 5

Alex and Nina sat at an outdoor table not far from the science library. The young GTF patiently explained chemistry.

"I think I have ADHD," Alex complained.

Nina nodded. "I think you lack the will for this discipline."

"Yeah, I hate this stuff."

"Then why study it?"

Alex twisted his pen. "So much pressure from my folks."

"I understand."

"Oh, yeah," Alex asked. "What are your parents like?"

Nina batted her eyes and looked down. "Kind, but strict."

"Can I see a picture?"

Nina pulled out her wallet and shared a photo of an elderly Iranian couple.

Alex shook his head and studied Nina's face. "You don't look like them."

Nina nodded. "Yeah, I was adopted. My mother died during my birth."

"I'm so sorry to hear that."

"It's okay. I love my parents. They raised me as their own."

"Do you have siblings?"

Nina shook her head. "What about you?"

"Not that I know of," Alex joked.

Nina didn't laugh and observed Alex sternly.

"You're kind of serious," Alex remarked.

"Yes, always."

"You almost remind me of my dad."

"How so?"

"You're so intense."

Nina nodded, but then asked, "Who is your dad?" She didn't really care, but wondered why Alex was so full of himself.

"My dad is the CEO of Steiger Pharmaceuticals," Alex responded proudly.

Nina exhaled deeply and confessed, "It's every chemist's dream to work there."

"You should come over for dinner and meet Dad."

"Alex, I think we should get back to thermodynamics."

CHAPTER 6

The years had affected Cindy. Her long jet-black hair suggested youth from a distance. However, closer examination, revealed a harshness due to an absence of fat.

Cindy insisted that her frequent visits to Stanford were out of loyalty for her alma mater, but her friends knew she was lying.

While marching toward the science library, Cindy gasped and dropped her scalding cup of coffee when she saw her son studying with a woman who looked eerily familiar.

Later that evening, as Alexander entered his parents' house for dinner, Cindy swooped down her staircase and demanded, "Who was that woman you were with?"

"Huh?" Alex asked.

"She was wearing a red scarf," Cindy clarified.

"You mean my chemistry GTF?"

Cindy leaned against the railing. Her eyes widened with astonishment as she exclaimed, "That's your teacher?"

"Yeah, you were the one who told me to hire a tutor."

"Yes, that's right," Cindy admitted.

Alex headed into the kitchen and grabbed a fresh moon cake from a red box on the counter. While taking a bite, he asked, "What did Maria make for dinner?"

Ignoring his question, Cindy ordered, "Do not see that woman again!"

"Geez, Mom, is it because Nina is Muslim?"

Cindy wanted to scream, *No! It's because she looks like my former nemesis and might be her daughter!* Regaining her composure, she settled for "I just think you should hire a male tutor."

"Kind of sexist."

"Alex, don't argue with me."

"Nina is very patient."

"I don't imagine you're very focused while studying with this woman," Cindy opined. She understood her son very well.

CHAPTER 7

The following week

Cindy and Amy stormed into Ben's office.

"Ben, you won't believe this," exclaimed an exacerbated Cindy.

"That I won't get any work done?" Ben asked irritably.

"Alex met a Lana lookalike," Amy screeched. Added weight over the years had given the Beijing native a softer more maternal look.

"What?" Ben asked with astonishment.

Amy fluttered around the office and swooned, "Oh, Ben, you should see Alexander and his new girlfriend together. Young love!"

Cindy bounced over to where Amy was gushing and slapped her friend hard with a magazine.

"Ouch," Amy squealed.

"Whose side are you on?" Cindy growled.

"Oh, c'mon Cindy, they reminded me of Lana and Aaron."

Cindy stopped for a moment and remarked, "Those two outcasts were meant for one another, so your analogy is way off."

"They were like a couple from an 80s movie," Amy continued.

Cindy rolled her eyes and joked, "Godzilla or the Blob?"

Ben interjected, "Please be serious."

"I rooted for Lana and Aaron to get together," Cindy confessed.

"Of course, because it would have ended things between her and Curt," Ben noted.

"C'mon, Ben, don't be cynical. Deep down, Cindy is a romantic," Amy gushed.

Cindy snorted. "Don't be silly. Lana and Aaron were social-climbing rats who belonged in the gutter."

"Cindy, don't you think you're a bit harsh?" Ben asked.

"Nope, those two were trash," Cindy insisted.

"Because they weren't rich?" Amy squealed.

"Their fathers were killers as were they. My son deserves better."

Changing the subject, Amy asked, "Whatever happened to Walker? I've always wondered if he and Lana ran away together."

Ben walked back to his desk and said, "I'll Google him." While running a perfunctory search, his face grew grim.

"What is it?" Amy asked.

"Aaron Walker shot himself in 2018," Ben replied. "His sister Trinity Walker Petersen joined a wrongful death suit against Steiger Pharmaceuticals. The action alleged that the antidepressants produced by one of our subsidiaries prompted his suicide."

"I remember that case," Cindy remarked. "It was dismissed for lack of causation."

Ben nodded. "Indeed, the doctor was partly to blame for his misdiagnosis."

"Nah, it's the patient's fault for not having better self-control," Cindy continued. "These losers abuse what is otherwise a perfectly good drug."

Cindy whispered, "I've always had this horrible

premonition …"

"What?" Amy demanded.

"That Lana would come back."

"C'mon Cindy, that's just guilt talking," Ben suggested.

"I do believe in fate," Cindy confessed.

"In that case, let things between Alexander and Nina run their natural course," Ben advised.

"But what if they fall in love and marry?"

"As long as you don't interfere, Nina will just be another conquest and Alex will move on."

"Ben, Nina could be Alexander's sister!" Cindy declared.

"Half-sister," Amy corrected.

"It doesn't matter," Cindy snapped. "If Nina Farzad is Curt's daughter then she stands to inherit at least half of everything."

Maybe more, Ben thought. *At the rate Alex was going, he'd easily get disinherited.*

"Maybe Nina isn't Curt's daughter," Amy suggested.

"Then we must make sure Curt never sees her," Cindy ordered.

"This is a small town," Amy joked.

"Curt already saw Nina at a conference," Ben shared.

"What?" Cindy shrieked.

"Last week Curt flew into my office insisting that he saw Lana," Ben replied.

"Then we've got to get rid of her," Cindy cried.

ANALYSIS

Aaron Walker

Aaron describes himself as a simple guy, but he's articulate, intuitive, and familiar with literary references: The Iliad, Pygmalion, George Bernard Shaw, and Old Testament stories.

In Part 1, Aaron is suffering a mental breakdown. In Part 4, Ben reveals that he committed suicide in 2018, around the time of his sessions with Dr. Lee, who was over-prescribing antidepressants manufactured by one of Steiger Pharmaceuticals subsidiaries.

In 2017, when Aaron is with Daniel, he appears confident and energetic. However, suicide victims typically contemplate death months in advance. Warning signs include gifting their possessions.

For example, at the airport, Daniel asks, "Aaron, why do you keep giving me stuff?"

At the bar in Hong Kong, Aaron asked Daniel to "groom" Trinity to attract Curt Steiger and raise funds for his new business. However, most likely, Aaron was planning his suicide and hoped Daniel would care for his sister.

Aaron teases Daniel frequently but seems to like him and acknowledges his somewhat privileged background.

Daniel Petersen

In *Firm Resolve*, little about Daniel's personal life was revealed. However, in *Firm Denial*, it's evident that Daniel's background is complex. Like Aaron and Lana, Daniel is culturally mixed. His mother is Jewish while his stepfather was not.

In Part 4, it can be deduced that Daniel must have married Trinity because her last name is Petersen.

Lana Hayaak

Having suffered severe brain damage, Lana more or less died in 2015. Her mind is childlike, even compared to the way she was at fifteen as portrayed in *Firm Resolve*.

Through Aaron and Daniel's flashbacks, we see Lana the way she was before her trauma.

After brain injuries, Lana expresses sorrow when the Chinese nurses abandon her. Subconsciously she is haunted by her past experiences. At fifteen, she woke to discover her parents gone.

In *Firm Denial*, Lana's mind is like a pre-teen. She speaks and thinks like a character from a novel she probably read as a child: *Alice in Wonderland, Wuthering Heights, and Jane Eyre.*

Nina Farzad

Looks like Lana, but is punctual, stern, and very passionate about chemistry, much like Curt Steiger.

Peter the Cat

Lana's beloved cat played a vital role in *Firm Resolve*. He was a constant source of discontent to Curt. The feeling was mutual as Peter expressed distrust for Curt.

The cat was also a clue regarding Lana's disappearance

as she would never leave without him. In *Firm Denial,* Peter is the only one she remembers. She barely dreams of Curt, and never thinks about Aaron or Daniel.

Incidentally, Peter genuinely liked Aaron. The feeling was mutual since Aaron rescued Peter and went to significant trouble to smuggle him into the United States and gift him to his sister, Trinity.

INTERPRETATION

Firm Resolve is told through the eyes of Lana Hayaak and sometimes Curt Steiger or Daniel Petersen. *Firm Denial* is mostly Aaron Walker's account of what happened between him and Lana. It's up to the reader to decide what actually occurred.

ABOUT LICIA FLYNN

Licia Flynn grew up attending international schools and obtained a Juris Doctor from a law school in Silicon Valley. Her undergraduate focus was political theory and military history.

On her maternal side, Licia is descended from Irish immigrants who arrived at the Port of New Orleans in the 1800s. Licia's paternal grandparents were educated merchants who fled China in the 1940s.

www.instagram.com/liciaflynn
www.facebook.com/FirmResolveLiciaFlynn
www.twitter.com/FirmResolve
www.klar-marketing.com

FIRM RESOLVE
By Licia Flynn

When an American couple vanishes in Kuala Lumpur, their teenager struggles to survive. Meanwhile, three entrepreneurs envision their Silicon Valley startup. Years later, the company relocates to Shanghai, and an executive's wife disappears.

Pre-order on AMAZON for 50% off until the launch date – 5/29/2018